NATURAL ENEMIES

ROAN PARRISH

Edited by Julia Ganis, JuliaEdits.com

Cover by Roan Parrish

GET "A RELUCTANT SANTA" FREE!

To instantly receive the free holiday romance, "The Reluctant Santa," as well as other exclusives, sign up for Roan's newsletter at **bit.ly/2xHGvBjF**

In memory of my grandmother, the plant witch of Parkside Avenue.

PROLOGUE

STEFAN

I WAS EATING at my desk as I had every lunchtime since I began working at Scion Laboratory two years ago. Most of my colleagues ate together in the courtyard in mild weather, or settled in groups of twos or threes in the cluster of chairs near the windows that looked out over Rockefeller Park and the Hudson River when it was too hot or cold to eat outside at the pier. But I didn't have anyone I particularly wanted to eat with. Or, more accurately, there didn't seem to be anyone at Scion who particularly wanted to eat with me.

Besides, it was convenient to catch up on emails at lunch. I had a system. I spent the morning in the lab, recording data and prepping samples. I caught up on emails at lunch, so they wouldn't distract me. Then I spent the afternoon in the greenhouse. I enjoyed going home with the smell of soil in my nose. In the evenings, I went for a jog, cooked myself dinner, read one article from *American Journal of Botany*, and went to bed. I'd had the same schedule since graduate school, so I always knew precisely where I was supposed to be and when. It soothed me.

And if my days were a bit repetitious, and my evenings a bit lonely, I could accept that. After all, I had a plan. I had goals. And sometimes to achieve your goals, you had to make certain sacrifices. That's what I'd been taught, and I believed it. It had worked so far, hadn't it?

———

THE EMAIL from Charlie came as I finished the last bite of my turkey sandwich with mustard on wheat and cleaned my fingers on a napkin from the stack I kept on my desk. I hated crumbs or grease on my keyboard. I wasn't an animal.

Charlie was a friend from grad school. We'd embraced a healthy attitude of competition that had propelled us both forward in our studies as students, but now, as professionals and colleagues, had taken on an edge of bitterness that I could identify, but didn't feel moved to discuss, because the bitterness issued from Charlie, and I was used to it. Getting one of the top jobs in your field, in a desirable city, the year you finished your PhD wasn't just enviable, it was the stuff vendettas were made of.

I clicked open the email lazily, expecting a pdf of Charlie's recently published article on bumblebee-mediated pollination of the Swedish *Orchis militaris*, or a silly meme. Instead, it was a link to *Time Out New York*. The message said: *Would've expected to find you on this list if I was going to find a plant guy at all...*

The link led to a list called "30 Under 30: Rising Stars in NYC," and I skimmed the pictures of carefully posed, smiling faces until one snagged my eye. In what had to be a candid photo, curly brown hair rioted around a man's high cheekbones and huge grin. He was half turned toward the camera, as if the photographer had called his name mid-laugh. He was beautiful.

To the right of the picture, it read:

2

Milo Rios, 28, Botanist. Rios is the Head of Programming at the Brooklyn Botanic Garden where he runs a botanical-themed story time for youngsters, curates the Learning Courtyard, and created a neighborhood planting initiative for local teens. Rios lives in Crown Heights, and says, yes: he has heard every joke about A Tree Grows in Brooklyn *you can imagine.*

I only realized I'd fisted my hands around my sandwich wrapper in rage when crumbs scattered my desk and keyboard.

"Programming?" I muttered. "Do you even need a degree for that?" My palms started to sweat and the back of my neck prickled.

Compared to other sciences, botany was nearly always overlooked. And to have a botanist featured in a highly visible publication—even if it was a lowbrow one—was huge. The kind of visibility that promotions and funding were built on. And the one time it happened, it wasn't me.

I was under thirty. My research into protein isoforms produced by alternative splicing had fundamentally challenged the dominant hypothesis that FLM-δ acted as a dominant-negative protein version. My research had been published in the *New Journal of Botany*, for god's sake, and they had even used a pop-out quote! In red. How could this kid from Brooklyn, who didn't even know enough to use a posed photograph, have been tapped as a 30 Under 30 rising star instead of me?

The anxiety crept up from my stomach to my throat, turning the taste of turkey to acid. The voice that had lived in my head for as long as I could remember started whispering.

It should have been you. If you were better, it would have been you. If you just did more, tried harder, were more, it would have been you. How embarrassing to be overshadowed by a glorified tour guide. You really don't have much to show for your work at all, do you?

I pressed on the center of my chest as if I could neutralize the acid with my fingertips. I'd gotten very good at calming myself down when the floods of anxiety hit. After all, I had a lot of practice. I might have gotten one of the most prestigious jobs in my field right out of grad school, but I'd paid a price for it. Success might be lonely, but I'd been lonely for a long time before I'd been successful.

Even as I swept the crumbs into my cupped hand and my agitated heart pounded in my ears, I found myself zooming in on the picture of Milo Rios. There was something about the man's grin that seemed mocking. He looked carefree and confident, as if he was happy exactly as he was.

I couldn't even imagine what that would be like.

"Who the hell are you?" I muttered at the screen. "And who the hell goes to a botanic garden next to a subway station?"

And then and there, sitting in my office of glass and steel, looking out over the lab I hoped to run someday, I decided I was going to find out. I was going to go to Brooklyn, and I was going to see what all the fuss over this Milo Rios was about. He couldn't be that perfect, right? He'd probably *tried* to get a prestigious job like mine and ended up at the botanic garden when it didn't work out. Chances were he was just as anxious as I was, only he was better at hiding it!

Yes, I'd go down there and see for myself that I'd made the right choices. That I'd ended up exactly where I wanted to be, even if I did spend almost all my free time working or worrying that I wasn't working.

It was just what I needed to remind myself that I was on track for the future I'd planned. It had absolutely *nothing* to do with Milo's dark curls or the way his smile fell like sunlight on a seed that had lain dormant deep inside me for years, nudging it to blossom.

Nope, nothing to do with that at all.

1

MILO

I LOVED to start the day with my hands in the dirt. It reminded me of why I'd fallen in love with plants in the first place—the textures and smells and promises of life. Now the ground was ready for my high-schoolers coming in tomorrow, and I still had time to grab a quick coffee from the snack bar before my eleven thirty tour. It was a perfect morning.

Saturday tours at the Brooklyn Botanic Garden were usually a mixture of families with young kids, tourists, and BBG members looking to eke every last drop out of their memberships, and I liked them because people were curious and relaxed. On a sunny but chilly late-March morning just edging into spring, I laid my bet on a small group of older couples taking advantage of the sun or visiting New York off peak tourist season.

Coffee chugged and hands washed, I found my tour group at the entrance to the garden. I'd been right about its makeup, for the most part. Four couples who looked to be in their sixties, two couples with five kids between them, and a tall, muscular white woman dressed in running gear who looked like she'd ducked inside on a whim and decided to take the tour.

Just as I was greeting the group, another man approached.

He had a runner's build, with broad shoulders, but he was dressed formally for a Saturday, in perfectly tailored, pressed gray wool pants. A charcoal collar and cuffs were just visible under a navy and cream wool sweater, and he wore a sensible lightweight jacket. He was black, with clean-shaven, flawless dark skin and close-shaved hair. I would've said he was hot, except that he had a sour, haughty look on his face, and I tried to avoid lusting after pretentious assholes if at all possible. I'd had enough of that in grad school.

"Are you here for the tour?" I asked.

The man looked me up and down like he was assessing something for purchase.

"Yes," he said, and he removed a small notepad from the pocket of his jacket.

I raised an eyebrow at that, but gave him the same welcoming smile I gave to everyone. Hey, some people took their leisure time hella seriously.

I ran through my welcome speech by rote, mind half on the planting session with the students from Erasmus High School the next day. They were a good group, and I was excited to see what they'd chosen to plant. One of them reminded me so much of me at that age, alive with the new discovery that I had the power to make things grow. It was heady and unfamiliar, especially coming from a neighborhood where things were more likely to wither than to grow.

It had been the most powerful lesson of my life: just because something isn't thriving, doesn't mean it can't, if given the opportunity. I'd been a gangly fourteen-year-old with warring impulses. Half of me had wanted to tramp through the streets of Crown Heights and sit in Lincoln Terrace Park all day; the other half had schooled me to smile less, feel less, talk less, and front more.

The accidental skid of my bike tire in the freshly spilled dirt of a jade plant that had tipped off a stoop had been the catalyst for everything I now held dear. If I hadn't taken the plant and the mendable shards of its pot home. If I hadn't superglued the pot together and replanted the waxy jade. If I hadn't kept it on the roof that summer, for water and sun. If I hadn't sat with it, looking out over my neighborhood and the city that lay beyond it... I'd never have become the person I was today.

The gift of nurturing something into being was one I deeply wanted to share with the kids I'd gathered. Because bringing something into being meant you could do the same to yourself, if you ever needed to.

I led my tour group down the path, past the fenced-in area I'd prepared this morning, and into the aquatic house, aware that the latecomer's eyes were on me as much as they were on the plants. Maybe he just wasn't that into the tour and needed something to kill some time?

"This is a Tiger Orchid," I told the group. "They're native to tropical Asia, and are considered the largest orchid species in the world. They only bloom once every two to four years, but they can stay in bloom for months at a time."

The man with the sour expression shook his head and muttered something to himself, scribbling intently in his notebook.

"Did you have a question, sir?" I asked, voice casual.

The man's expression flashed uncertainty, then he muttered, "*Grammatophyllum speciosum.*"

"Yup," I confirmed, and gestured to the plaque that listed the Latin below the common name for the orchids. I waited for a question, and when one wasn't forthcoming, I continued with the tour, holding back an eyeroll. It was annoying, but every now and then I got one of this type who fancied himself an expert because he'd memorized the *Encyclopedia of Plants and Flowers*. I usually ignored them. I'd learned a long time ago that getting angry punished me far more than them.

There was a sweet lady who was visiting from Montevideo

and was an avid gardener, so I concentrated on her instead. She asked halting questions, until I spoke to her in Spanish as we walked, and then she bubbled forth with anecdotes of plants from her own garden and grinned up at me when I joked about hiring her to come work with me. I concentrated on her for the rest of the tour, trying not to look at the man I'd dubbed Pretentious Assface in my mind.

I led the group through the Japanese gardens, where Pretentious Assface asked an esoteric question about an obscure variety of the Japanese Clock Flower. Then through the bonsai museum, where Pretentious Assface corrected my pronunciation of Fukinagashi, the windswept style of bonsai. I gritted my teeth and fisted my hands in my pockets, because in addition to making my day worse, getting into arguments with guests was also strictly forbidden.

I always ended the tour at one of my favorite sections of the garden.

"These are pretty cool," I told the group. "They're Sensitive Plants. Sometimes they're called Prayer Plants, or Humble Plants, or Sleeping Grass, or Touch-Me-Nots. Watch and you'll see why."

I bent close to the plant and stroked my finger along it. The thin, splayed leaves furled together at my touch, the plant curling in on itself.

There were the usual exclamations from the tour group, and I smiled. It always felt like the plant and I were doing a magic trick.

"You can try," I told them. "Touch the plant, or pinch it gently."

I moved out of the way and watched as each member of the group played with the plant, some in delight, some in surprise. All of them smiled as they stepped away. All of them except Pretentious Assface.

Pretentious Assface spared the plant half a glance, but didn't touch it. He muttered, "*Mimosa pudica.*"

The irritation I'd kept mostly at bay finally bubbled up and I squared off with Pretentious Assface.

"Yes, the Latin name for these, if any of you are interested, is *Mimosa pudica.*" I took a step toward Pretentious Assface, whose eyes were narrowed. Then I spoke quickly, letting the irritation creep into my voice, looking directly at him as I addressed the group.

"Its foliage undergoes nyctinastic movement, meaning the foliage closes under cover of darkness, or in response to seismonastic movements, such as the stimuli of touch, warmth, or vibration. Those stimuli are transmitted from the point of stimulus on the leaflet, to the leaflet's pulvinus, to the pulvini of the other leaflets, and then along the leaflet's rachis, then into the petiole, and finally to the stem. Potassium ions flow from the vacuoles of the pulvini's cells, causing water to flow from them through aquaporin channels by osmosis, which makes them lose turgor. This folding costs the plant a great deal of energy, and interferes with photosynthesis. Scientists believe the trait evolved as a defense from herbivores, with the logic that animals might fear a fast-moving plant, choosing to eat a less active one instead. Additionally, the sudden movement might serve to dislodge harmful or predatory insects."

The group was looking at me with glazed eyes and eyebrows raised at this sudden surge of aggressive science.

"*Mimosa pudica* is also sometimes referred to as Shame plant," I said, speaking close to Pretentious Assface's ass face.

The man's eyes widened. But not with anger or shame, like I'd expected. He looked...stricken. He bit his lip and looked at the ground, folding into himself as surely as the Sensitive Plant had. I stepped back, guilt warring with irritation.

"Uh," one of the fathers said, while trying to keep two children from punching the Sensitive Plants, "do any of the other ones do anything cool?"

I appreciated even his clumsy attempt to break the tension.

"What, you mean besides converting radiant energy from the sun into chemical energy?" I winked at the man's kids. "Photosynthesis," I explained. "Well, nothing quite so cool as the Sensitive Plants, but these over here smell pretty good."

I led the group to the lemon basil and chocolate mint planted nearby, calming myself down with the familiar scents. I'd tended every one of these plantings at one time or another and I brushed gentle hellos to their leaves with my fingertips.

As I ended the tour near the entrance where it had begun, I fielded a few final questions about what we'd seen and, as always, about people's home gardening woes. Pretentious Assface was strangely quiet. He hadn't so much as muttered anything since the Sensitive Plants.

Now, though, he was peering at me out of the corner of his eyes as he pretended to study the BBG brochure. I took a few deep breaths, waved as the tour group scattered, but Pretentious Assface was still there, peering.

"Hey, man," I said. "Can I have a word?" Then I walked to a slightly less public spot next to some boxwood hedges.

The force of annoyance that had been building during the whole tour—all the mutters, the corrections, the sidelong glares, the judgment—exploded. I was used to being muttered at, used to people taking one look at my worn jeans and messy hair, or my brown skin, and assuming I didn't know what I was talking about. I was used to glares and judgment too. I'd gotten them my whole life. But I'd be damned if some stranger was going to come into *my* garden, treat me like I was trash, and ruin the tour for everyone.

When the man joined me, I squared off with him, glared and snapped, "Okay, can I help you with something, or what?"

"What?" Pretentious Assface said, shifting from foot to foot and avoiding my eyes.

"You paid money to take this tour and you clearly didn't get what you were looking for. You made that real fucking clear by muttering shit and rolling your eyes. So. Is there some information about the fucking garden I can provide for you, or are you just an asshole?"

The man's eyes went wide for a moment and then his face turned to stone. "I guess I was expecting a bit more, that's all," he said. "From a fellow enthusiast."

What the hell did that mean? "Uh, who are you?"

"My name is Stefan Albemarle," the man said, and for a moment it seemed like he was going to extend his hand out of sheer knee-jerk habit.

"Is that supposed to mean something to me?"

"Clearly it doesn't," Albemarle sniffed. We stood awkwardly for a moment, and finally Albemarle said, "It just wasn't very informative. The tour. You didn't discuss the plants' functions in their natural landscapes, designate which are members of the same families to show the ways similar traits display differently. You didn't even see fit to share the Latin names of the plants or how they were discovered."

"Dude, it's not a tour for botanists and horticulturalists! It's Saturday morning. You *saw* who was there. It's a tour for people who think gardens are cool, or who are interested in learning surface-level shit about a topic. Tourists. Families looking for an activity. Besides, clearly anyone—like *you*—who already has a thorough knowledge of those things doesn't *need* to be told them." I glared. "Why *are* you here, anyway?"

Albemarle sniffed again and examined his watch, then smoothed his sleeve. "I just don't think there's any harm in giving through, detailed information."

"Yeah, I didn't say I thought giving more info was going to

cause an outbreak of measles or anything. I said people don't want that info. It's boring to non-specialists."

Albemarle's eyes narrowed and his shoulders squared at *boring*. "I wouldn't think an *expert* would find such things boring." He said *expert* like it was in scare quotes.

"Are you hearing the words I'm saying?" I was generally pretty laid back, but my temper was fraying. "This is not a tour for experts, even though, *yes*, I am one. This is a tour for laypeople." My hands were fisted at my sides and I was glaring. "But since we're on the subject, real expertise is knowing your subject matter so well that you know what information is relevant to communicate in what contexts and to what audience. Real expertise is recognizing when some things won't matter to people outside your little circle of specialists. Real expertise means being able to make people *care* about something because you present it in an engaging and relevant way! I love what I do and I love showing it to people in a way that might make them love it too."

Albemarle's eyes were wide, his mouth slightly open. Shocked? Angry? I couldn't tell and at this point I didn't give a shit.

"So, I guarantee you I can answer any damn question you have about any damn plant in this garden. But don't come on my tour and ruin it for everyone else—who, by the way, paid the same money as you and have the same right to enjoy the tour— by being a total dick!"

With the word *dick* delivered right to Albemarle's face, I turned on my heel and stalked away.

2

STEFAN

I PACED AROUND MY APARTMENT. I'd already gone for a jog, but it hadn't leached off any of my fidgety energy. Five miles, and still all I could think about was that I'd been lectured by a glorified tour guide.

I snorted in disgust and stared out the tall living room window. In the distance, the *Quercus palustris* and *Prunus x yedoensis* were filling out lushly as spring took hold. With deep, measured breaths, I forced myself to calm down. Every year I watched these trees move through the seasons, the cycle as dependable and predictable as the moon.

The deepest satisfaction in my life was seeing the patterns that governed the world. The simple, stark mathematics behind the glorious bursting forth of flower and leaf. It was the only thing I could depend on. People weren't governed by any such patterns. They were unpredictable. Unknowable.

And it wasn't as if I hadn't tried. I'd spent my early teenage years following the patterns that were laid out for me. Act *this* way because that's how my neighbor acted. Like *that* music because that's what the kids at school liked. Have *those* goals, because they were the ones people expected of me.

So what if the things that were expected of me didn't

resonate with my true desires? At least when I pretended, I wasn't so alone. It was worth it. For a while, anyway.

By the time I was in high school, though, I'd realized I wasn't very good at pretending. More importantly, I'd realized it wasn't just the things I liked or the things I wanted that made the other kids treat me like a pariah. It was something intrinsic.

So I'd stopped fighting it. I'd turned away from the world as I knew it and set my sites on a new world.

Expectation wasn't determination, I'd told myself over and over. Not for good or for bad.

College had been better, but not as different as I had imagined. I'd pictured a utopia of people like me. But even there, something had set me apart.

Something deep and essential and unexciseable.

I had thrown myself into my work, cloaking myself in lab hours and final projects and internships and accolades until years had passed in a slipstream of achievement and isolation. And in that sea of isolation, I grasped at my achievements like icebergs—solid, bracing, undeniable.

I shivered, and went to make dinner. On the train home from the botanic garden, I'd decided that what had irritated me the most about my encounter with this Milo Rios was that the man was clearly intelligent and capable, but was perfectly happy to pander to people as opposed to educating them. He had a captive audience on his tours; he had the chance to open up the whole world of botany to them, and he squandered it on cutesy stories and gardening tips that anyone could look up for themselves.

But as I lost myself in the meditative repetition of chopping and slicing, other thoughts crept in. I had gone there to remind myself of how good I had it. Of how satisfied I felt with my own choices and where they'd gotten me. That just because someone I'd hardly even call a botanist had gotten the kind of public accolades that I never had, I was still better off.

I'd gone there to prove all that to myself. And I hadn't.

The other guests on the tour had loved him. They'd watched him with fascination and enthusiasm. They'd nodded and laughed and thanked him before leaving. Yes, they'd loved him for doing hardly anything. I tried every day to do *everything* and no one had ever responded to me with anything approaching that level of enthusiasm.

It wasn't fair. No matter how much I did, how hard I tried, how great my accomplishments...none of it ever got me what Milo Rios received from total strangers on any given Saturday.

A mirror had been held up to reflect what I already knew: people just didn't like me. They liked him, and they didn't like me. It had always been true, but realizing it all over again hurt just as much as ever.

That night, I dreamt of flying. I soared over a field of *Papaver rhoeas*, then zigzagged down, chasing a glorious smell. I alighted on the source of the smell. It was comfort and nurturance and solace. I basked in it, until it closed around me, my iridescent wings shredded by the *Dionaea muscipula's* teeth, my armored carapace crushed and consumed.

As the flytrap closed, there was a moment of panic, but then it was gone, and I was held again. This time, though, it was a man's arms around me, holding me tight. Not destruction but contentment; not consumption but appreciation.

In the flash of dreamtime between sleeping and waking, I glimpsed the man's face. The wide brown eyes, wild riot of dark brown curls, and lush mouth were those of Milo Rios.

"Damn," I muttered. Why couldn't the guy at least have the decency to be unattractive?

Refusing to allow something as undependable as dreams to influence me, I took a cold shower and put the vision of Milo out of my mind.

All day, though, as I did my weekly grocery shopping and prepared the week's lunches, my mind returned to him. I got more irritated with each intrusion. I couldn't keep thinking about him. It was torture. By nightfall, I'd determined that I needed to do something to purge Milo from my system.

I hated that he'd gotten the last word and I hadn't said my piece. He had no idea who I was or what I did, and maybe if he knew, he'd understand why it mattered so much to me that people hear about the amazing world of botany—the only world that had ever welcomed me. The only world that meant anything to me.

So, what I needed to do was go back to the Brooklyn Botanic Garden and have the last word. Explain. If I could make Milo understand, then I could stop thinking about him. Stop thinking about the way the sun glinted in his hair, and what it might feel like to wrap those curls around my fingers. Stop thinking about how those work-roughened hands might feel against my skin, or the way those crooked teeth would scrape against my—

Yeah. I really needed to have that last word.

———

I SPENT the next few days at work deciding which of my creations would drive the point home best. The point, of course, being that there was more to botany than being a tourist attraction—it was all about innovation and experimentation and discovery! The point was also, secondarily, that Milo had been rude and infuriating and annoyingly attractive and I needed to get the upper hand because...well, because I *did*. I couldn't have his face in my head as I went about my business. It was distracting. Really distracting.

After work on Wednesday, I boarded the train to Brooklyn, genetically engineered blue chrysanthemum in hand. I shielded it from being jostled not because it was delicate, but because I took care of the things that I valued.

I crossed Flatbush Avenue quickly, buzzing with adrenaline. I'd say my piece to Milo and then this would be done with. No more intrusive thoughts of the man, no more agitation, no more dreams. I could return to my peaceful life and my work and that would be the end of it.

The tree-shaded brick archway was in shadow as the light grew dim, making it look like the entrance to a secret garden. As I stepped through the revolving iron gate, it struck me how different Milo's life must be from mine, working in a place like this.

"Hello. One, please," I told the man at the ticket booth.

"I'm sorry, sir, but we're ten minutes from closing. We stop admitting patrons half an hour before."

"I don't need time to see anything. I simply need to speak to Milo Rios."

The man looked unmoved. "It's policy, sir."

"Could you make an exception?" I kept my voice calm and low. I'd found it was far more likely to get me what I wanted. "I just need a moment to speak with Milo. I'm happy to pay the full admission anyway."

"Ah, well..." The man dithered. He was white and looked to be in his mid-seventies. Most likely a volunteer. Probably not terribly invested in the letter of the law. "I guess maybe, if— Oh, Milo! Great timing."

I spun around to find Milo a few feet away. He was holding a shovel, and his work boots and the knees of his jeans were dirty. He only wore a T-shirt despite the chill in the air and his strong arms gleamed with sweat. The easy smile slid off his face the second he saw me, and I felt an unexpected pang of disappointment.

What might it be like, just once, to be the cause of someone's smile instead of its disappearance?

Milo's eyes narrowed and I drew myself up to my full height. Milo raised an eyebrow and leaned deliberately on his shovel. "Did you need something?"

"Just a word."

"Does it have to be in Latin?" Milo drawled.

Before I could respond, the man in the ticket booth said, "Ah, go ahead in, sir."

Milo turned sharply and strode away, as if he was sure I would follow, just as he had the first time we met. It forced me to jog after him like a dog or a little kid and my resentment grew.

"Okay, shoot," he said, once we were inside a fenced-off area. He dug the tip of his shovel into the earth, clearly picking up where he'd left off, as if I weren't even there. I stood on the pavement just inside the fence. A rain of soil sprinkled my shoe and fury reared in my gut.

"Excuse me!"

"You afraid of a little dirt? Cleanest stuff on earth."

"That's...not true at all."

Milo rolled his eyes and leaned on his shovel again. The look he raked me with was evaluative. When his gaze reached the spray of dirt on my shined shoes, he snorted.

"Look, if you came all the way here again to report me to my supervisor, she's not working today, but I can give you her email. Or if you're here to call me out, just do it. Hell, we could have a formal duel with gardening tools if you don't want to get your hands dirty. But whatever you're here for, can we move it along? Because I have shit to do."

Suddenly it crashed down around me and I felt utterly foolish. What was I doing here? I'd come to get the last word, to get him out of my head, but I had no idea what that last word should be. After all, we'd disagreed over the ideal content level of a garden tour. Was I really going to—what? Rattle off the contents of my CV and current research? While he shoveled? Jesus, what had I gotten myself into? I inched backward. What if I just left? Milo would probably never find me. I'd never have to see him again. Surely he'd get out of my head eventually, right? Sometimes the best move was retreat.

"Yo, seriously. You got something to say, or what?"

Milo was paying attention now. He dropped the shovel and approached. I found myself holding out the plant I'd brought like a shield between us.

"I came to tell you..."

Humiliation flooded me. I couldn't do it. This had been a terrible idea. Possibly my worst idea ever.

I shook my head. "Never mind. I, uh. Here." I thrust the pot at Milo, and turned to flee.

Then I heard a crash.

"Shit."

I turned back toward Milo slowly, my heart pounding. My chrysanthemum—my beautiful blue chrysanthemum lay smashed on the pavement, its roots naked in the weak sun. My stomach lurched into my throat and I immediately dropped to my knees and scooped it into my hand.

"Shit, man, you don't just shove stuff at people!" Milo scolded, but he looked stricken. He took off, and returned a moment later with a clean terra cotta pot the same size as the one that smashed. "Here. What kind of soil was it?"

I brushed soil from the chrysanthemum's petals. "Loamy, with a pH of 6.5."

"Sure. C'mere." Milo led me to a table just inside a temporary enclosure, and indicated a bag of soil.

I spooned soil into the pot and nestled in the roots. I added more soil mixture, anchoring the seedling.

"You're okay," I told it, swallowing hard when I realized I'd said it out loud in front of Milo.

Milo leaned in and peered at it, his nose wrinkling adorably. "So, uh. What is it? I mean, it's a chrysanthemum, obviously, but..."

I drew my shoulders back and straightened my spine. "Yes. I spliced in the genes of the *Clitoria ternatea* and *Campanula medium,* which are naturally blue, shifting the chrysanthemum's acidity level to catalyze the color change."

I allowed pride to infuse my voice. Finally, I felt like I was stepping back on solid ground. Talking about my work was comfortable, familiar.

"Ah, gotcha. You're one of those." Milo nodded knowingly, and gave the plant a last look. "That's cool."

Then he walked back outside, leaving me and my chrysanthemum in the potting shed.

I stalked outside a moment later to find Milo digging again.

"One of *what,* exactly?"

"Huh? Oh. You know. A plant eugenicist."

What I did could accurately be termed agricultural eugenics. I didn't care for the term, but many in the field used it. But when Milo said the word it was dripping with scorn. His tone said: snob, elitist, pretentious. It made worse accusations.

My humiliation transmuted to anger at his judgment so fast I got a headrush.

"Let me guess," I snarled. "You argue that weeds are just as beautiful as flowers and think you'll change the world with rooftop gardening."

"What's your problem with rooftop gardening, bro?"

He stepped into my personal space, nostrils flared, clutching the shovel.

"What's your problem with eugenics?" I blurted. Milo's eyebrows rose so high they disappeared under his hair. My words caught up with me and I cringed. "I mean...damn it."

"Oookay, anyway."

"I didn't mean that. Obviously I know what the problem is with eugenics. I just..." I trailed off, feeling my face heat. Milo was looking at me like I was absurd, pathetic, ridiculous, and that was exactly how I felt.

"Why did you come here, man, seriously? What is this?"

This close, I could see the flecks of amber in Milo's brown

eyes, could see the softness of his lashes and the way one of his front teeth was in front of the other. A curl of his hair hung over his forehead and he had a smudge of dirt on his chin. As I watched, his eyelids drifted half shut and I found myself completely unable to look away. I was frozen to the spot and my heart began to race.

"Unless," he said slowly, stepping right up to me, "you didn't come here to talk shit at all. Maybe you came here for something else." His gaze dropped to my mouth and he bit his lip. "Nothin' to say now?"

I blinked madly, trying to sort things into brand-new categories. Was Milo...hitting on me?

I took a step backward as Milo stepped forward, then another, as if we were dancing. Then my shoulder blades hit the fence and Milo was so close I could smell him—fresh soil and sunlight and the sweetness of light sweat.

We were the same height, so when I looked at Milo, he was looking right into my eyes.

"What's it gonna be, Stefan?" Milo's voice curled around my name and it felt like a hand around my cock I was so suddenly turned on. I took a shuddery breath and Milo's mouth curved in a knowing smile. "Huh," he said. "That right?"

I closed my eyes and bit my lip. I was so hard and so mortified. How could this be happening? Things like this did *not* happen. Not to me.

Milo leaned in close and I opened my eyes to see hunger in his expression.

Then he was kissing the hell out of me, mouth hot, tongue slick, a hand at my throat and the other sliding up my back to drag us together.

A shot of pure lust blasted through me and I grabbed at Milo too, squeezing his hips and pulling us together. My head fell back against the fence as he fed on my mouth and I heard myself cry out as his hand slid down to my ass.

I felt like I was dissolving into velvety heat everywhere we touched—mouth and throat and ass and groin—and suddenly it was too much. It had been so long since anyone had touched me. I was so close. I was going to come.

I wrenched my mouth away to suck in air, and shoved Milo away. In my desperation to ease back from the edge, though, I shoved hard. I watched helplessly as Milo, suddenly off-balance, sprawled on the ground.

"What the hell, man?"

My head was spinning, my heart pounding, and every nerve ending thrumming. All my signals felt scrambled, overloaded.

"I'm sorry— I didn't mean— Are you—"

Milo stood up, frowning, but I couldn't stand another moment of feeling like this. Wrong. Pathetic. Ridiculous. I had to get out of here.

Milo called after me, but I didn't even hear it over the blood rushing in my ears as I ran. Ran from the first person who'd made me feel something in years.

3

MILO

I WAS HELPING Troy Avilla drag a huge, leaking bag of soil onto the wheelbarrow to take out to the plots allocated to my outreach program with the Erasmus High students

Troy reminded me of myself as a teenager. A little hopeful, a little suspicious, and a lot unsure of his place in the world. In the weeks since the program for Erasmus students had begun, Troy had blossomed alongside the things he'd planted, and I was already thinking of trying to get him in for a summer internship.

My phone buzzed in my pocket, and I hoped it was Laura Mancino returning my call about the lot on Nostrand. I was working on a proposal to turn it into a community garden sponsored by the BBG. It was probably just my sister-in-law, Mariana, though, and I would see her later.

We finally wrestled the bag into the wheelbarrow. Troy nudged my shoulder. "That dude's grilling you."

I pushed my hair off my face with the heel of my hand and looked up to see Stefan Albemarle hovering on the path outside the greenhouse.

It had been almost a week since our encounter, which had ended with me ass-down in my own dirt after a hot as fuck kiss. I wasn't sure what the hell had happened. One second, Stefan's mouth was hot and slick under mine, his hands grasping at me, and the next, I was falling and Stefan was looking at me in horror.

"All right, you got this?" I asked, indicating the wheelbarrow. Troy nodded, shoulders squared like he could take on anything. His protectiveness made me smile. "I'm good, man. Finish this up and then take off. I'll see you next week."

Sweat slid down my back and my hands smelled of earth. Stefan was dressed as impeccably as he'd been the last two times I'd seen him: another pair of pressed wool pants, these in light gray with a pale blue check, and a sharp, geometrically patterned navy and red sweater. His full lips looked soft and lush. I swallowed hard, because now I knew firsthand that they felt as soft and lush as they looked.

Stefan's hands were clasped behind his back, putting his firm chest on display. He looked like he'd never touched dirt in his life. I wanted to get him dirty. No: filthy. Wanted to see him panting and sweating and begging and—

"Hello," Stefan said as I approached.

"Didn't think I'd ever see you again."

"Oh, I...well. I, um. I left my chrysanthemum, so..."

Stefan worried his lower lip between his teeth and looked at the ground.

"I thought that was a gift," I said softly. Stefan's eyes flew to mine. He looked awkward and stiff, and I wanted to kiss the shit out of him all over again.

"It was meant to be. But I, uh. I never told you how to take care of it, so I..."

"Course. You *had* to come back. Couldn't have me killing the only blue chrysanthemum in the New York Metro area." I smiled, but it seemed like Stefan couldn't identify a joke without a microscope.

"One of five, actually."

"Aha."

We stood, facing each other as the silence turned uncomfortable. Usually, I would've smoothed it over. Joked, or made small talk, or asked questions. I could talk to anyone. It had been a survival skill growing up in a neighborhood filled with such different people. Fly under the radar, blend in, and if you stood out, make yourself easy to get along with.

But something about Stefan made me not want to fill the silence between us with the same easy talk I could have with anyone. I wanted to see what he would say.

"I just wanted to check on it. I didn't want you to do the wrong thing," he said finally.

I rolled my eyes. "You do get that I'm a botanist, right? Like, attended school, know about biology, botanist. I *chose* to apply my knowledge here; I didn't end up here because I failed to do something else."

"Still, you couldn't possibly have experience with this particular strain."

His words were dismissive, but he ran a hand over his chest, as if checking for stray lint or specks of dust. A nervous gesture that said even though he seemed self-possessed, he hadn't always been that way. A gesture that said his concern for the plant was anxiety, not scorn. The anxiety of a man who was used to people letting him down, used to not being able to trust anyone.

A pesky warmth kindled in my chest. The kind I felt for under-watered plants and too-crowded vegetable patches and dogs left tied up outside bodegas, straining at their leashes.

"Well, let's go," I told him. "We can check on it, and you can make sure I know what to do. If you let me keep it, that is?"

Stefan's eyes widened, like he wasn't expecting assent, and he nodded quickly. "Yeah, of course. You can keep it. If you really want it."

I smiled. That was really almost adorable. I slid my hand

into Stefan's and pulled him toward the greenhouse where I'd left the mum.

Stefan studied it closely, running a gentle finger along the surface of the soil to check its moisture content.

"It looks fine," he said, finally, sounding incredulous. "You did fine."

"Yeah, well, like I said. I know my shit. It's a chrysanthemum so I watered it like I would a freaking chrysanthemum. It might be blue, but it's not that complicated." I pointed at myself. "Botanist."

Stefan clasped his hands behind his back in what must've been his habitual stance. "I apologize if I offended you. I have a tendency to be...a bit..."

I raised my eyebrows when the rest of the sentence wasn't forthcoming. "Of a pretentious asshole?" I supplied. I kept my tone kind.

Stefan's eyes flew to mine. "Yeah. I suppose so." His voice sounded defeated and sad. And though I'd wanted to take him down a peg after the tour, I found I didn't like hearing it that way. I didn't like it at all.

I dragged the toe of my boot on the ground between us. "Hey, listen. The other day. The kiss. I didn't mean to freak you out."

"I wasn't."

I snorted. "Really. You shove people you're making out with into the dirt and run away when you're fine? Hey, I guess it takes all kinds."

"No, I just— I apologize. I didn't mean to hurt you."

That shuttered, formal speech made me want to shake him until the mask of it fell away.

"You didn't hurt me," I said, and caught his arm. "Tell why you ran away. If you wanted me to stop, you could've just—"

"I didn't!" Stefan's eyes burned into mine, and his nostrils flared. "I didn't want to stop."

"Then what? What were you so scared of?"

"I... I was..." Stefan picked another invisible something off his sweater and I had the sudden urge to take his hands in mine so they couldn't find any more fault. He cleared his throat and when he spoke it was choked. "I was afraid I was going to come."

All the blood rushed to my groin and I got hard so quickly I felt lightheaded. My groan made Stefan shudder and look away. "Jesus. Would that have been so bad?"

Stefan shrugged. "It's just been a while."

"Well, shit, it was a pretty good kiss for someone who's rusty."

When his eyes met mine again, they were burning with shy pleasure. "Just pretty good?"

I shrugged and turned away, but I was pretty sure he could see my grin. "Ya know. Not the best I've ever had."

Stefan grabbed my shoulder and spun me around. "I like to be the best at things."

I slid my arms around his waist. "Yeah, I'm kind of getting that."

Our mouths met in a pulse of hot sweetness. Stefan tasted of coffee with sugar and his tongue curled around mine in a dark dance. I spun us and pressed him against the wall, dragging our bodies tight together, so close I could feel the pulse of his heart against his chest.

Stefan gasped and fisted my shirt. I pressed kisses to his jaw, and when I sucked on his neck, he shivered.

"Stop, stop, oh god," he gasped. He pushed me away with straight arms, like we were teenagers dancing awkwardly, and hung his head, breathing heavily.

"Oh fuck, are you gonna come?"

He was visibly hard, his erection pressing obscenely against the beautiful wool of his trousers. He whined and it sent a flush of lust through me.

"I want to watch you come," I said into his ear. "Fuck, I wanna watch you make a mess all over these fancy clothes."

Stefan shuddered, eyes fluttering open.

"C'mon." I dragged him through the glassed-in walkway to the indoor rooms, weaving through groups of afternoon visitors and past a woman who'd set up an easel to paint the *Echeveria* 'Afterglow.' I unlocked a back door that led out to a greenhouse that wasn't open to the public.

As soon as we walked in the air changed. It was warmer in here, and the smell of life was thick on the air.

"Oh, wow," Stefan said. "Is that a *Tacca Chantrieri* —mmph."

I slammed our mouths together, kissing him deeply, feeling his taut body become pliable against mine. I bore him backward against the wall, and pressed us so close together we both gasped for breath. His heartbeat pulsed against my lips as I sucked at the juncture of neck and shoulder, and there it was again—that sweet shiver, like his skin couldn't contain him.

Stefan grabbed at my shirt and I opened my eyes for a moment to see that his eyes were squeezed tightly shut.

"This okay?" I murmured, sliding my hand down his flat stomach to his crotch. He was so fucking hard. He groaned his assent and I fumbled at his pants, the hidden hook and eye closure of his fancy trousers taking me a moment. Finally, I dragged them down over his hips, revealing royal blue boxer briefs that glowed against his dark skin, and his straining hardness trying to escape from them. "Fuuuuck," I muttered. "You're so hot."

He shook his head, but his eyes were ravenous where they rested on my hand cupping his cock. I slid my other hand around and squeezed his ass, the tight swell perfect in my palm. His cock jumped and he pressed his hips toward me.

"Mmm, can I suck you off?"

Stefan made a broken sound and nodded so vigorously I almost laughed. Stepping close one more time, I kissed him deep and long, rubbing his erection through the softest boxer briefs I'd ever felt. Clearly, Stefan liked nice things. He moaned into my mouth and his arms came around me, keeping me close.

A hedonist. Stiff and well-armored, he spread out in the warm sun and bloomed.

I kissed his cheek. Then I dropped to my knees and peeled that hot underwear down. His cock sprung out, gorgeous and rigid against his belly, and I licked it from base to head. Stefan slid a hand into my hair, his fingers so gentle. I looked up to find him watching me like I was a miracle. Like he'd never seen anything like this before.

I licked around the tip, tasting the sweet and salty musk that was Stefan's alone, and his whole body shuddered. His fingers tightened in my hair, but only for a moment.

"It's okay," I told him. "You can pull a little. I like it." He opened his mouth, but didn't say anything. He slid his other hand into my hair though, and I felt a tingle at my scalp.

I put my mouth on his dick, learning its dimensions, relishing its hardness and the feel of smooth skin against my tongue. I got him wet and then slid up and down, tonguing his head on the upstroke until his hips started to jerk.

I squeezed his ass and he groaned desperately. A lightning bolt of lust shot straight to my cock. *Oh yeah.* I would fuck that ass next time, no doubt. I cupped his balls and he cried out, his hands tightening in my hair as his balls tightened in my hand.

"Oh god, please, please," he started to chant. I dove back down his dick, sucking him deep, and felt the moment his control snapped.

He whined and grabbed my head, thrusting desperately, and I swallowed around his erection. He froze for a moment, then yelled as he came down my throat in hot pulses. I held him in my mouth until he shuddered a final spasm of orgasm, and then he whimpered and collapsed forward, hands on my shoulders.

"Oh my god," he whispered. His hand was back in my hair, stroking gently. "Thank you." He sounded so sincere I almost laughed.

I got to my feet and moved in to kiss him, pausing a breath from his lips, in case he didn't want to taste himself on my tongue. But he closed the distance between us and enfolded me in his arms, kissing me avidly. His kiss was desire and gratitude and welcome, and it made something deep in my stomach go wobbly with affection. Then he ran his palm down my throat and my lust reasserted itself.

I was achingly hard, my cock pressed against my waistband from the way I'd been kneeling. I ground myself against Stefan and he caught me by the hips and held me close.

"Sorry," he murmured. "Do you want me to..." He glanced down at my crotch and all the easy relaxation his orgasm had imparted dissipated. He bit his lip.

"No," I said, running my thumb over his lip to rescue it from his teeth. "Will you just touch me?"

His eyelashes fluttered and I noticed how long they were, with a sweet curl to them. He relaxed again and undid my jeans. As soon as he touched me, I bucked into his hand, the delayed pleasure catching up to me in a head-spinning rush. I fell against him and let him take my weight.

We kissed and he stroked me and my whole body felt held in a suspended moment of pleasure. Then Stefan squeezed a little harder and started twisting his hand, and I was coming undone. Liquid heat washed over me and I shoved my tongue deep in his mouth, wanting it to last forever. He jerked me fast and hard and my orgasm tore through me, clenching every muscle. I shot in hot pulses against Stefan's stomach, my hips jerking, mouth open on a silent scream against his neck.

As I came down, little shudders of pleasure zinged through me as Stefan ran gentle fingers over the tip of my dick, slippery with release.

"Uhhhhh, god," I groaned, sagging against him.

I chuckled at the picture we would've made if anyone came in, two grown men plastered against a wall, spent dicks out, surrounded by tropical plants in various stages of germination.

I pressed a kiss to the skin just under Stefan's ear and disentangled myself. As we pulled our pants up and put ourselves back together, he made a noise of displeasure.

"Oops," I said, as he dabbed at my come on his sweater. He shot me an unamused look that tickled me. "Hey, I did say I wanted to make a mess of your fancy clothes."

His eyes flashed with heat and he looked down.

I watched him for a minute, watched his ears show a touch of pink at the tips. "You like it," I murmured.

He shook his head. I tipped his chin up so I could see his face; his jaw was tight.

"Mmm." I leaned in. "You like the idea of me messing up your perfect, expensive shit, hmm? Coming all over it. Making you come in those nice wool pants." He shuddered and his eyelashes fluttered. "Mhmm." I patted him firmly on the cheek. "Here." I stripped my T-shirt off and wiped at his sweater. It was warm in here, so I'd be fine in my undershirt.

"It's okay," he said, and took his sweater off. "It, uh, needs to be dry cleaned anyway."

I smirked at him and slid down the wall to sit on the floor. Now that I'd come, I felt pliant and sleepy. Stefan sat next to me.

"That's right," I said, sliding a hand up his thigh. "Get your pants even dirtier." I heard his breath catch, which was exactly why I'd said it.

We sat in easy silence for a while, then Stefan bumped my

hand with his. He tried to play it off like it was an accident, but his eyes kept darting down to my hand.

"You're a little bit adorable with how you have no game whatsoever."

Stefan froze and spluttered and I shook my head and took his hand. "This what you wanted?" He sighed and nodded grudgingly, but his hand in mine was tense. "I'm serious. It's pretty fucking cute. You're all proper and perfect posture and pretending you came here to check on a damn plant."

"I *did* come here to—"

"No." I swung around to face him, throwing a leg over his and leaning close. "You came here to get my tongue back in your mouth and my mouth on your dick. Maybe you couldn't admit it to yourself, but I could see it the second you looked at me today."

"H-how did I look at you?"

"Like you wanted me to shove you around and do shit to you. Like you hoped I would make the move so you didn't have to." Stefan looked down and swallowed hard. "Like you wanted me to push you to your knees and fuck you until you came all over yourself." He gave a strangled sound and squeezed my hand so hard it was almost painful. "Mhmm." I leaned in and kissed him slow and deep. "Next time."

"Jesus."

He shivered again, still clutching my hand, and I eased back down beside him and decided to let him off the hook.

"So, why do you like rare plants so much? Just because something's rare doesn't mean it's better."

Stefan considered that for a moment. "No, not intrinsically. But to be able to do something that hasn't been done before—to make something that only exists halfway around the world? It's so...special."

"I can see that." I dropped my head against Stefan's shoulder and looked at the greenhouse around us. With my gaze soft and unfocused I could almost imagine I was home, my own plants all around me. "I guess for me, it's more about finding specialness in stuff that's ordinary. Or seeing a flower I've seen a hundred times before, but this time it's in my neighbor's window and I see it in a new light because I know my neighbor chose it specially, out of all the other flowers they could've chosen." I shrugged. "Maybe I just have simple taste."

Stefan was staring at me intently, eyes shrewd and considering. "I always liked unusual things, I think. Maybe because I always felt...a bit unusual."

"You didn't fit in," I murmured.

"That's an extreme understatement," Stefan said. It was an attempt at lightheartedness, but his expression was anything but lighthearted. He picked an invisible speck of dust off the wool stretched over his muscular thigh and I slid my other hand over his to quell the nervous gesture.

"Like how?"

"I was just never what people expected me to be."

He bit his lip and my eyes were magnetized to his mouth. Before I'd touched him, I'd wondered if he would kiss with the same precision he seemed to apply to everything else. Now I knew his kiss was like a dam of control breaking on the rocks of desire, unbounded and messy and necessary.

"I never liked the right music or the right movies. I didn't talk right. Or, rather, I talked too right. You know, there are just...stories of how the world expects black men to be. What we're supposed to like."

I nodded. I knew all about stories like those.

He sighed and his grip on my hand loosened a little. "I didn't like the things the other boys in my neighborhood liked. I didn't like rap or R&B, and I wanted to watch movies they thought were stupid. White people shit, they always said. 'Why you all about that white people shit, Stef?' 'Why you tryna talk

33

so white, Stef?' 'You think you better than us cuz you actin all white?'"

His voice was bitter, mocking, but when he spoke again, it was small.

"And the kids who were into the stuff I liked never really accepted me, like they thought...I don't know. I tried for a while. To be what everyone seemed to think I should be. I thought something was wrong with me that I didn't. But it felt like acting, you know? I could do it. I could play that role. But it wasn't me. And...probably I didn't really do it as well as I thought I did. At least, not well enough that anyone wanted much to do with me at school, or in my neighborhood."

I swallowed around a lump in my throat. "What about now? Like, at your lab and stuff. With your friends. Can you be yourself now?"

"I..." He shook his head. "No. That is—" He slid his hand out of mine self-consciously. "I don't really have many— Um. When I'm myself people still don't like me. They think I'm..."

He broke off and bit his lip, eyes cutting to me, and I cringed. "A pretentious asshole. Shit, man, I'm sorry." I brought his hand up and kissed his knuckles, like my mouth could soothe the hurt it had caused.

"Yeah." He shrugged. "But...I think maybe I am. I don't mean to be, but..." He shook his head in frustration.

I could see how it had happened. A kid who never felt good enough, never felt accepted. He probably clung to the things he *was* good at, the world that accepted those things about him. And academia rewarded achievement, elitism, rarity. It was a macho beast, and if you let it, it could chew up everything in you that didn't value what it valued. Conforming was a survival mechanism.

"I get it. It's just your thorns. But in a non-hostile environment, maybe you could disable the defense mechanism," I said.

Like before, when I was going down on you and you blossomed for me.

A bark of laughter startled me, and Stefan's usually stern expression cracked into a sweet grin. I smiled back at him.

"You know, just because you work in a fancy plant eugenics lab"—he elbowed me—"doesn't mean you can't still have some fun."

"I thought we just did."

"Did you just...was that a *joke*? Ladies and gentleman, observe this exceedingly rare species in its natural environment —the never before seen *joke*—"

Stefan tumbled me onto my back and knelt over me, shutting me up with a hand over my mouth. I licked his palm and watched his eyes go sleepy. He bent down, but when he kissed me his lips were soft, just a promise. Shit, he was really sweet.

"My point," I said, pushing us upright, "is that you should come hang out here next Sunday morning. I'm doing this program with some kids from Erasmus. We met a few times and talked about growing conditions, particularly in an urban landscape, and about the uses of certain plants. Then each of them evaluated the environment of their own neighborhood and decided what would be the best thing to plant there. A few of them chose garden mums, spider plants, and purple waffle plant because of the way they can clean the air. They live in neighborhoods that aren't served that well by the sanitation crews, so they thought it would make a positive difference. Well, I think also they just loved that there was a plant called the purple waffle, but. Others are growing vegetables because produce isn't easily available in their neighborhoods."

Stefan was watching me with interest, rubbing his thumb absently against my thigh.

"A couple are doing really bright flowers because they think that beautifying their neighborhoods will make people happier, which could potentially lead to less littering and crime—did you read that article comparing the happiness of people in different cities based on green space access and cleanliness?"

Stefan shook his head. "Which journal was it in? *Green Infrastructure*? I missed a month last year."

Wow, he was ridiculous and a little bit adorable. "It was in an obscure little journal called *The Atlantic*."

He ducked his chin. "Oh."

I chuckled. "So, once they've experimented with growing their chosen plants here, we'll find places in their neighborhoods to put them. This one kid, Abraham, decided he wanted to grow something ugly because he didn't want to make all the weeds and stuff that were already growing in his neighborhood feel bad by comparison."

I winked at Stefan.

"That's...a joke, right?" he said finally.

I looked at him for a minute. Took in his perfectly put together outfit, his posture, even when sitting, his perfectly groomed hair. "Is it?"

4

STEFAN

"MORNING, EVERYONE," Milo said. "This is Stefan and he's gonna hang with us today. He's kind of into plants too." I opened my mouth to correct him, but he winked at me, and I just swallowed hard. *Right, a joke.*

After he got the students set up, he took me around so they could tell me about their projects. A tall, broad-shouldered boy that Milo called Troy was working so intently in the dirt that he hardly looked up as we passed by him. Milo didn't bother him, just squeezed his shoulder.

"Where are you going to plant your vegetables?" I asked the girl next to him who was planting brussels sprouts, cauliflower, kale, and onions.

"There used to be this little community vegetable patch down the street that was hella old," she began.

"It was started in the seventies, Sonja," Milo said, shaking his head at her.

"*Anyways.* Some ice cream place opened and they got it shut down for literally no reason. Stupid. So there's a lot near my house where I want to try and start a new one," she said. "Milo's gonna get it for me, right?" She turned shining eyes to Milo.

His face told me there was more to the ice cream parlor story than "literally no reason," but he just said, "I'm trying. It's a zoning issue, though, remember?"

Sonja rolled her eyes. "That's so stupid. It's just sitting there full of trash and, like, pee. Way better as a garden."

I waited for Milo to explain the law to her, but he just nodded sympathetically and said, "It *is* stupid. Most of the barriers to repurposing land for green space are legal. And because this city is a seething bureaucracy, even if you *can* get stuff done, it takes forever for it to happen."

Sonja made a face and Milo nodded.

"I've got a call in to the Land Trust Alliance, though," he said. "You'll know when I know. And if we can't use that lot, we'll figure something else out. I promise we'll make this happen."

"If you say so," Sonja said, flipping her braids over her shoulder, but I could see her smile as she turned away.

A tall white kid wearing a yarmulke was glaring at his phone on the other side of the planter.

"What's up, Abraham?" Milo asked.

"I still can't decide. None of these are that ugly." He held up his phone to show a picture of English ivy.

Apparently Milo hadn't been kidding about this.

He didn't meet my eyes. "Everything near where I live is ugly. I hate how my street looks. It's all cars and puddles and trash. But..." He fidgeted with his phone then slid it back into his pocket and shrugged. "It's home. I don't wanna make it look uglier by planting something really pretty. Ugly by comparison, you know?"

I waited for Abraham to smile, but he looked totally sincere.

"You know what's kinda ugly, but in a cool way?" Milo asked. "Ferns."

My head shot up. He had to be kidding. "What? Ferns

aren't ugly, they're amazing! They're fractals! Self-similar, iterated, mathematical constructs! They're anything but ugly!"

Abraham raised an eyebrow at me and looked at Milo, who was looking at me with amusement. He took Abraham's phone and clicked around.

"Tell me those things aren't ugly as hell." He held up Abraham's phone to display an image of fiddleheads."

Abraham peered at it. "So ugly. They look like alien fetuses."

"Those are not *ferns*," I insisted. "Fiddleheads are furled fronds that haven't even grown into ferns yet!"

"Yup, fetuses." Abraham nodded.

I gaped at them both. I couldn't believe Milo would betray ferns like this. Milo laughed and squeezed my shoulder, which sent warmth coursing through me even in the face of his betrayal.

"Here, check these," he said, showing Abraham something else. "They look like weirdo fingers or something, so people wouldn't think they were super pretty, but when there's a bunch of them together they just look green and nature-y."

"Maidenhead ferns," Abraham read, looking at the phone. "Oh. Those are ugly. Like fucked-up lace."

We left him contemplating ferns, and Milo led me to a boy and a girl who had run a long orange extension cord into the garden and attached it to a blender.

"Is that a...dirt milkshake?"

Milo laughed. "Yeah! It's good for you. High mineral content. Great for pregnancy." He winked.

"Wait, what?"

He put his hands on my shoulders and leaned in. For a moment, I thought he was going to kiss me again, in front of everyone. I looked around wildly to see who was watching us, embarrassment at war with desire. But he just looked me dead in the eyes and said, "I am fucking with you. C'mere."

When the blender stopped, Milo said, "This is Rooney." The white girl with red hair nodded at me. "That's Deon." The short black boy gave me a mock salute. "Would you guys show Stefan what you're doing?"

"Moss smoothie," Deon said.

"Makes moss art," Rooney added. Milo was grinning.

"Okay, so we've been working on getting the right consistency," Deon explained. "If it's too thin it just drips. Too thick and it's all clumpy. But this should be about right. You wanna do it?"

Rooney nodded and smiled at him, grabbing a paintbrush. She took the blender over to the wooden fence and began painting the mixture onto the fence. She worked slowly, wiping away drips as she went. She explained, "The moss is blended with yogurt and water and sugar. We can spray it with water to help it grow."

When she stepped back, she'd written *Rooney + Deon* with a big heart surrounding the words.

"Aw," Deon said when she smiled at him. "Our love immortalized in moss. So romantic."

"Some mosses can absorb liquids up to twenty times their own weight and distribute them uniformly," I said.

"Yeah, there you go." Milo hooked his arm through mine. "Liquid absorption, the height of romance." But he smiled at me and squeezed my arm close to his side.

"It is, actually," I told him. "The power of a strong relationship is that it can take on more than either person could on their own, right?"

Milo's eyes narrowed, but he nodded. I didn't know where the words had come from.

———

THE ERASMUS STUDENTS left at two, and Milo crowded me against the fence, next to the edge of Rooney's moss heart.

"So, you gonna come home with me?"

My heart started to pound. This close, I could see the flecks of gold in his dark eyes, and the way his stubble outlined the curve of his upper lip. I let my gaze linger on his mouth long enough that he smiled. I'd wanted to kiss him since the moment I'd arrived this morning. A part of me had even wished he would kiss me hello when he'd met me just inside the front gates.

Now, I let myself lean in and take his smiling mouth in a kiss. He slung a casual arm over my shoulder and settled into the kiss. Everything about him was casual, easy, relaxed. I couldn't even imagine what it must feel like, but it made me want to stay close in the hope that I might absorb some of that ease.

"You look hot today," he murmured against my mouth, tugging on my shirt. He'd told me to wear clothes I could get dirty in, but his text had contained so many winky emojis that I hadn't been sure whether he meant the literal dirt of the botanic garden or...something else.

I'd split the difference, wearing dark green twill pants and a navy button-down with a maroon stripe.

"Like, 'preppy guy I want to debauch' hot," he went on, kissing my neck above the collar of my shirt. His tongue flicked out and a shiver of arousal ran through me.

"Yes," I said.

"Mm?"

"Yes, I'll— Oh god," I moaned when he slid his hand down and squeezed my erection. "I'll come home with you."

"Great," he said, giving me a firm stroke that weakened my knees, then pulling away. I steadied myself with a hand on the fence and took a deep breath.

As we walked east from the BBG, Milo pointed up one street and down another and told me about the projects he'd done. There was a snap in the air, but the afternoon sun made leaves shine and brick seem to glow. Or maybe that was just because I was with Milo.

"Hey, Mrs. Portillo," he called, slowing down.

An elderly woman sitting in a lawn chair on her stoop waved at him and we stopped in front of her house. "Hello, dear. Who's your friend?"

"This is Stefan. Stefan, this is Mrs. Portillo. Stefan works with plants, like me."

"Ma'am," I said. She smiled at me.

"Emilio, dear, if you have a minute, would you mind?"

"No problem. Cilantro and mint?" She nodded. "One sec," he said to me, and went to the side of her brownstone. Tires were stacked, three and four high in a neat line against the side of the house. Milo ran his hand over the herbs growing in the first tire stack and pinched off a handful of mint. He did the same with cilantro from the third tire, and delivered them to Mrs. Portillo, who patted him on the cheek.

"Gotta run. I'm gonna show Stefan my garden." He grinned at her. "Save me some food?"

"You got it, sweetie."

Milo tugged on my hand like an overgrown puppy and pulled me down the street.

"Nice to meet you," I called behind me.

"You too, dear."

Milo was almost bouncing with excitement as he turned the corner a few houses down and pulled keys out of his pocket.

"Emilio?"

"Yeah. When I was born, my brother couldn't say Emilio, and it became Milo." He shrugged. "Just kind of stuck."

"It suits you."

"Yeah? How come?"

Because it sounded lighthearted and happy and buoyant and sexy. "Because it's the name for a puppy," I said.

Milo laughed and pushed the door open. "I've heard it before."

I followed Milo up stone steps that had been worn in the middle from years of climbing. I forced myself to imagine the amount of pressure and friction required to erode stone; the relentlessness of human banality that stripped away the very stuff of nature. I forced myself to imagine that to keep myself from staring at Milo's round ass clenching in worn denim as he climbed in front of me.

"Did you plant those herbs?" I asked.

"For Mrs. Portillo? Yeah. I, uh." He ran a hand through his messy curls and glanced back at me. We had reached the top floor and he led me down a dim hallway. A bare bulb flickered ominously. "I met Mrs. Portillo when I was thirteen. She had these marigolds on her stoop. The kind they sell in September at the grocery store, you know? Her husband had brought them home for her but they were dying."

At the end of the hallway, Milo unlocked a scarred wooden door.

"Come on in."

I immediately lost the thread of his story as I stepped over the threshold. Because I felt as if I were a storybook character, stepping through the door of one world and entering another.

My first impression was that Milo's apartment was alive. Plants covered the walls and climbed across the ceiling. Plants hung from ropes and lined shelves. Plants crawled across windows and clustered on sills.

"Oh my god," I breathed.

"Yeah." Milo closed the door and encouraged me inside with a hand at the small of my back. "It's kind of a lot, I know. I didn't exactly mean for it to go this far, but once people knew I had plants, I just kind of ended up with them whenever people didn't want them anymore, or they got too big, or they started to die. You wanna see?"

He sounded almost shy.

"I definitely want to see."

His grin was immediate and so sweet it made me ache.

He showed me around the apartment, pointing out certain plants of strange province. The rubber plant he'd found in a jumble of belongings on the curb with a sign that said *I DON'T WANT ANYTHING THAT SCUMBAG TOUCHED*. The lacy philodendron he'd found outside his front door with no note at all, that must've come from a neighbor.

There was a fiddle-leaf fig plant in the corner that he'd ordered for a customer when he worked at a garden store years before that had never been picked up, and an ivy cutting from a friend's housewarming party that had taken over the half-wall that divided Milo's bed from the kitchen during a particularly warm summer three years back.

The tiny kitchen had boxes of spider plants, verbena, and jasmine on top of the refrigerator with leaves spilling down its sides. Along the wall to the left of the stove, Milo had affixed boards studded with mason jars, each full of herbs. In the corner of the kitchen was a hanging planter of chives, chamomile, and...

"Is that catnip?"

"Oh, yeah. I dry it for my friends who have cats. And...well, I'll show you after."

The windowsill in the living room held a cluster of beautiful, geometric glass terrariums that housed silver nerve plants, golden club moss, and button fern. The afternoon sun striking them threw dancing light across the opposite wall.

"My friend Johnna makes them," Milo explained.

In the bathroom, succulents sat in a box on the toilet tank and air plants hung on the wall over the toilet. Next to the freestanding white tub, a worn wooden ladder was propped against the wall, holding a towel and several aloe plants. The brick wall behind the shower was visible through the transparent plastic shower curtain, and I could see where Milo had removed a few of the crumbling bricks and planted mosses in their recesses. A moss bathmat lay just outside.

Every square inch of Milo's apartment had been cultivated with care. It wasn't only the plants, either. In such a small space, with plants taking up so much space, and needing so many different things, he had made a home for every single one of his belongings. Found a place for them, or created the space around them.

Even with the sounds of the city buzzing in the distance, it was an oasis. It was the most intentional, peaceful place I'd ever been.

His bed rested on the floor, and a small pallet was his bedside table. Even there, leaves grew between the slats, growing toward Milo's pillow. Yearning toward him. I understood how they felt.

"This is... I've never seen anything like this."

Milo chewed on his lip. "You get it, then? I know it's a lot, but it's..." He shrugged helplessly, looking around. "They're mine, you know? They're me. I give them what they need to grow and then they *live*. I breathe out anger or fear or exhaustion, and they take it out of the air and give me back something green and sustaining and..."

He trailed off self-consciously. This was who he was. He was too many plants in a tiny space. Plants called to him because he took care of things, nurtured them, gave them what they needed to thrive.

I felt oversaturated—so full of feeling I almost didn't recognize myself.

"Yes," I told him. "You understand that each one needs something different than the one next to it. You respect those differences. You give each what it needs and you enjoy the way it grows."

My voice wavered. When was the last time I spoke to someone who saw me? Who understood?

Milo crossed to where I stood near the bed. He cupped my face and looked into my eyes. "I do," he said. "It's good that they're all different. It's okay that they're the way they are."

His gaze was intense, and when his palm landed on my chest, over my heart, I gasped. Everything about him electrified me.

"I like that they want certain things," he said, eyelids half closing as he slid that palm down my stomach and cupped my cock. I hardened in his hand and he leaned close. "I like the specificity. It's what makes them what they are." His grip tightened and I hardened further. "I like giving it to them." He cupped my ass with his other hand. "I like giving them what they want. What they need."

He pressed with both hands, squeezing my ass and my erection, and my whole body felt hot and needy.

He took my earlobe between his teeth. "Do you want that? Do you want to let me give you what you want?"

He bit down sharply and I slammed my hips forward without meaning to, trying to get more friction.

"Stefan." His voice was flower petals and pollen and honey. He traced the shell of my ear with his tongue and it made me shivery and lightheaded.

"Yes, I— Oh, god, yes, I want it."

"Good," he purred, then his mouth claimed mine in a bruising kiss and his hands were everywhere.

He pressed me down onto the bed and stripped off my pants. He unbuttoned my shirt and threw it over his shoulder where the sleeve snagged on the outflung leaf of a philodendron. It looked like the plant was waving to me with my own shirt.

"You're so gorgeous when you smile," he said, pulling my undershirt up to reveal my stomach. "It changes your whole face."

He pulled the shirt over my head but twisted it so my hands

were caught above my head, resting against the wall. The trailing leaf of the fern tickled my knuckles as if it too was saying hello. As if everything in Milo's world was welcoming me here, now.

Milo straddled me, leaning in to kiss my neck avidly, and I arched into him. He groaned as our erections ground together, and I almost came off the bed. The heat and pressure of his body against mine, the sucking bites to my neck, his tongue in my mouth—it was so intense I was right on the edge again.

I rolled away, dragging in a breath. "Just gimme a minute," I managed to get out. Milo's hand pressed between my shoulder blades, and his stubbly cheek followed.

"You okay?" he asked softly.

I wasn't okay. I felt like I was coming apart every time he touched me. And I was more okay than I'd ever been. I shrugged.

He kissed my back. "How long has it been, babe?"

I tensed and he squeezed my shoulders, thumbs digging in on either side of my spine, forcing my shoulders to drop.

"A long time," I said. I didn't need to be any more specific than that.

"Okay. Well, you're in luck. Because you need to be touched." He dug his thumbs into a knot beneath my shoulder blade. "And I really fucking like touching you. So it works out."

He eased me back down on the bed, on my stomach, and kept working the tense muscles of my back.

"Chill for a bit, okay?"

I nodded. With my face buried in his pillow all I could smell was him. Something light and fresh and woodsy, with a musky bite beneath it.

He slid my boxer briefs down my thighs, dropping a kiss at the base of my spine.

"God damn," he muttered as he bared me. I got a playful pat on each ass cheek and a bolt of lust shot through me as I pressed

47

my hips into the mattress, the drag of the sheets along my cock lighting me up.

I heard the sounds of him getting undressed, and then he was back, straddling my ass, the heat of his naked flesh shockingly intimate. He ran a hand down the back of my neck, and then started kneading my muscles again.

"So anyway, Mrs. Portillo's marigolds were dying," Milo said, voice low and lulling. "And it was right after I'd discovered that I could make things grow. I started watering them for her, and I loosened the soil, and they came back to life. And every day I'd walk past her stoop and I'd see them, and it made me happy. I started doing the same with other people's plants after that. Watering neglected window box herbs, and re-potting things that had outgrown their containers. All over the neighborhood. And I really thought I was like Batman, you know. A mysterious vigilante, rescuing plants under cover of night in the city of Gotham."

His fingers moved to my lower back and he relaxed muscles I hadn't even known were tight. The pressure on my hard cock trapped against the mattress made me squirm to try and get some relief.

"Mmm," Milo said, running a hand between my legs to fondle my balls.

I cried out and ground harder against the bed.

"Of course, it turns out, I wasn't Batman." He started kneading my ass, holding my cheeks in his hands and parting them, so I felt the cool air touch my hole. I shuddered. "Turns out, Mrs. Portillo had seen me watering her marigolds through her window, and my other neighbors had just let me be since I was thirteen and thought I was the shit."

He chuckled. Leaning over me, he kissed down my spine, murmuring words against my skin between kisses.

"I guess I just never stopped. I loved that I could make things bloom in a neighborhood that didn't have that much green space. Loved making people happy. Such a little thing, a plant. But it's like hope in a pot."

He kissed the base of my spine, and then he kept going. His stubble grazed my ass and then his slick tongue flickered against my hole and I shot off the bed so hard I was worried for a moment I broke Milo's nose.

I twisted around to face him—he had one hand cupped over his face and reached the other to my knee. "Okay, should've warned you. My bad. You okay?"

"I'm so sorry. Are *you*?"

"Yeah, no harm done." He grinned. "You want to let me back at that sweet ass, or no good?"

Heat washed through me and a broken sound escaped my lips.

"That's a yes, right?" he said, eyes on the precome that slid down my erection at his words.

"I'm just a little...on edge."

Milo touched the tip of my cock with his finger, circling the head as he watched me. I gave up another bead of precome at his touch and fisted the sheets.

"You're so sensitive," he murmured. "'S so hot."

Then he touched the tip of his tongue to his finger and tasted me.

"Oh my god."

"Do you get how hot it is that you're on the edge of coming from one touch of my tongue? One touch of my finger? Come whenever you come, babe. I'll think it's hot. Come once, come a hundred times. There's nothing about it that I won't like. Now lie your hot ass back down and let me taste you."

All the air went out of me. If it was true that I could just feel what I felt and let my body do what it wanted to do, and Milo would like all of it...

I dragged in a deep breath and blew it out slowly. Milo

kissed me, then pressed me back down onto my stomach. "Can you..."

"Hmm?"

"Can you hold me down? I'm afraid I'm going to...hurt you again."

Milo groaned. "Can I hold you down while I fuck you with my tongue? Yeah, it's a real hardship, but I'll do what I can. Jesus fucking Christ," he muttered. He spread my ass cheeks and pressed me firmly into the bed. "I think you can do your worst now, and there's no escape," he said.

Before I could even process that, the heat and slickness of his tongue was right there, and I was shivering as my nerve endings fired and fired again.

He circled my hole, licking and sucking until I was shaking beneath him and grinding my hips into the bed. Then his tongue slid inside me and I nearly screamed.

"Mmm," he moaned against my ass and I felt the vibrations inside me.

"Oh god."

"Do you wanna come like this?" He trailed rough fingertips over my swollen balls. "Or you want me to fuck you?" His rough palm caressed my inner thigh. "Or you want to come like this and then get fucked?" He licked my hole again. "Whatever you want, babe."

I felt like I was floating on a cloud of pleasure and the slightest move might let me fall through. I tried to speak and it came out like a whine.

"You want me to decide?" he asked, and I nodded, so relieved I slumped into the mattress. "I can do that," he drawled.

He kissed lazily down the inside of my left thigh and up the inside of my right.

"I think..." He spread my legs. "That I want to fuck this ass until you're screaming." He gave me a spank and every muscle in my body tensed. "Yeah." His palm soothed where he'd just hit.

He pushed my right knee up, spreading me open for him, and rolled my balls in his hand. I writhed and looked back over my shoulder at him.

He shot me a searing grin as he rolled a condom on. My eyes were glued to his erection. To Milo's hand stroking lube over himself absently, eyes on me, sleepy with lust.

"How do you like it?" he asked. My eyes shot to his. "You know what? Never mind." He slicked his fingers. "My decision, right? I'm gonna do you however I want."

I buried my face in the pillow again, nodding once I couldn't see Milo anymore.

"Mhmm." He pressed a steadying hand to my lower back and then I felt slick fingers slide inside me. "I'm gonna do whatever I want with this."

"Yes," I hissed as his fingers slid deeper, opening me up.

A few fumbling hookups in college. One depressing encounter with a married neighbor whose eyes always followed me. A hand job in the gym shower. It had all left me with a sour taste in my mouth. Sex was a reminder that there was something wrong with me; that I would never feel satisfied; that even with men who wanted me...nothing ever felt right.

But Milo... Milo felt so incredibly right and I didn't know why. The way he touched me, the things he said. His smell and the feel of him. It didn't even seem like the same act. The times before made me feel like I was nothing. This? This made me feel like I was everything.

"Milo." My voice cracked. His slick fingers moved inside me so sweetly.

"Yeah, babe. How're you doing?"

I had finally come to life.

"I want you," I managed to choke out.

"Mmm, good, cuz I want you too."

I tensed nervously when I felt his cock press against my hole and forced myself to relax.

"It's okay," Milo said. "I got you."

He moved so slowly it was almost like he wasn't moving at all. But then he breached my muscle and slid inside and we both groaned. There was a flash of discomfort and then he was pressed deep inside me, opening me up. He dropped his forehead to the back of my neck.

"Okay?" he gasped. I nodded. "Fuck, you're so fucking tight, feel amazing, shit," he mumbled.

I groaned and pressed back into him, feeling him that tiny bit deeper inside me. Milo growled and grabbed my hips, pulling out and slamming into me. He shoved me up the bed with the force of his thrusts and I braced against the wall so I could push back. We found a rhythm, then, hard and fast, and something inside me felt like it was unspooling as a dark, hot pleasure tore through me.

Milo bit down on my shoulder and something snapped. I tipped my ass up to change the angle and then every thrust of his hips felt like I was about to come. I scrabbled for purchase in the wreck I'd made of the sheets. Milo took pity on me and pulled me up on my hands and knees, holding my shoulders to anchor me.

"Touch yourself," he growled. I started to reach for my dick, but then he started pounding into me and I didn't even need to. The angle, the pressure, the slick fullness, it all coalesced into something huge I was standing on the edge of.

I squeezed my eyes shut so tight light burst behind my eyelids, and clenched my ass around Milo's length.

"Fuck, fuck," he chanted. He rolled his hips in a circle and I dropped my shoulders to the bed, unable to stay upright in the onslaught of sensation.

Milo shoved deep inside me and I was gone, pleasure detonating deep in the pit of my stomach and in my balls, and exploding through me like fireworks. My hard cock pulsed and I grabbed it, jerking myself off furiously as orgasm swallowed me.

Milo was saying something, filthy words tumbling around me like jewels, but I couldn't understand them through the ringing in my ears and the tingling pleasure that had consumed me. He thrust deeply a few more times, and each time I clenched down hard on him, my body responding even though I was wrung out.

Milo came with a strangled "*Fuuuuuuck,*" and collapsed on my back.

When he pulled out, my heart fluttered in fear. Would he want me to leave? Would he want to act like what happened was no big deal? But as soon as he got rid of the condom, he rolled us onto our sides and spooned up behind me, draping his leg over my hip and his arm over my stomach. My heart rate slowed and I inched back tentatively, away from the wet spot I'd made, and deeper into his arms.

"Damn," Milo moaned into my neck. "You about killed me. Your ass about killed me."

He kissed my shoulder and heat of a very different kind than I'd felt while he was inside me took up residence in my chest.

5

MILO

I SLOWLY SURFACED from a peaceful sleep. When I went to stretch, though, I found I was all tangled up with someone.

Stefan.

It all came flooding back as I shook off sleep, and my dick tried to rise to the memories. Fuck, Stefan's tight ass had felt better than anything. And the way he'd writhed and thrashed in my arms, like he couldn't get enough, like it was almost too much. Yeah, damn, that had done good things for my ego.

Now, I opened my eyes to find that he'd turned toward me in sleep. Our legs were tangled together, and he was holding my hand in both of his, face still peaceful, eyes closed in the fading light.

He looked so vulnerable like this. In my bed, holding on to me, breathing deeply. I couldn't resist touching him with my free hand. The line of his cheekbone, the curve of his eyelashes, the plump of his lower lip. When I touched his mouth he stirred, and I leaned in to kiss him awake.

His mouth parted under mine and he squeezed my hand, waking with a luxurious moan. Yep, hedonist all the way. And he was letting me be the instrument of his hedonism. It made

54

me hard as hell, even though I'd recently come so good it felt like I'd turned myself inside out.

We kissed lazily for another minute, then he pulled away.

"Hi."

"Hey." I smiled at the tension in his face. "You're a pretty nice thing to wake up to." The tension disappeared immediately and he smiled sweetly. Man, did I have a thing for his smile.

I rolled closer to him so I could reach a hand around and appreciate his ass again. Lying on our sides, facing each other, I was struck with how usually, by this point in a date, I'd want the other person to take off so I could get back to my day. I rarely thought about their smiles or the way they smelled. I rarely thought about them at all, and I certainly didn't crave them again after we finished. It was always casual, always just chill.

But I didn't feel chill about Stefan.

I would never have become friends with him or locked eyes with him at a bar. Somehow, all the things that made us so different also captivated me. Like within him lived a whole other world I had never given much thought to. And all I felt was content here, like this, with him.

I leaned in and kissed him again and my erection dragged against his hip. Well, okay, content and horny.

"Shit," I said. "I'm seriously hard for you. Damn, what'd you do to me?" But I winked and smiled at him. His eyes widened and he looked down between us. He was hard too, and when he looked back at me, his pupils were blown wide.

I inched closer to him, pressing us together, and watched his eyelids flutter, then close. His hand landed on my hip, and he flexed his hips, gasping. Fuck, he felt amazing.

"Mmm," I murmured, closing my own eyes and taking up his rhythm. I loved lazy, half-asleep sex. We moved together slowly, and I just enjoyed the friction, my arousal ratcheting up slowly and without urgency. Then Stefan's hand slid from my hip to my ass and he squeezed, and dragged me closer, my swollen cock crushing against his.

With that one move, *no hurry* became *I want to get off right the fuck now*, and I grabbed his ass in turn. We thrust harder and faster against each other, and his mouth found mine. He bit my lip, moaning as he lost rhythm and I took over. I flipped him onto his back and lay on top of him, rutting against him until he was crying out, head thrown back as he came.

I bit at the vulnerable line of his throat and he convulsed against me. The hot slick of his come was all over me, and I reached between us to jerk myself off. My orgasm was wrenching, Stefan's hands on me dragging it out like I hadn't come in weeks. As the pleasure tore through me, I buried my face in his neck, shouting as I came all over his stomach and his spent dick.

Our come was mingled all over Stefan and the sight of it made my cock give a last, desperate pulse.

"Jesus Christ." My voice was shaky, but I was strangely energized. I moaned into Stefan's neck and then kissed his mouth. "You okay?"

He looked like a different person. His eyes were sleepy with satisfaction, his mouth curved in a half smile, and his expression relaxed. He was so beautiful like this. In my bed. Covered in come.

"Yeah. I'm great."

"I am also great," I said around a groan as I stretched. He yawned, and his eyes fluttered shut. "You wanna sleep a little more?"

"Sorry. No, I'm okay. I've just been busy lately. With work. I've been putting in a few hours a night after dinner and going in early."

That was exactly the kind of schedule I'd wanted to avoid. It was a necessary evil in grad school—the all-nighters and cram sessions. But it wasn't any kind of life. Not if you liked to breathe fresh air or have relationships with people.

"Sounds stressful," I said, running a hand up Stefan's arm.

He nodded. "I just want to do a good job. I like to double-check things. Be sure."

All sorts of responses were on the tip of my tongue, like *You know there are things beyond work, right?* And *When do you have time for a life?* But I was pretty sure the answer to both was that Stefan didn't have much beyond work. Either he only cared about accomplishments, or it was all he thought he had to offer. I'd lay money on it being the latter.

"I'm sure you do a good job," I said, and kissed him softly. He had *so* much more to offer. He smiled against my mouth and leaned closer. "You wanna see my secret garden?" I asked.

"Is that...a euphemism?"

I laughed. "Nope. Legit actual, non-euphemistic garden." I pointed to the window out to the fire escape.

"Yeah. Let me just, um..." He looked down at himself.

"I told you I'd make a fucking mess of you," I said, and he shivered. "Here." I grabbed some tissues and cleaned us both off.

I went to take a piss and when I caught a glimpse of myself in the mirror I found I was grinning like a fucking idiot. I shook my head at my reflection. "You're ridiculous," I told it.

Stefan was fully dressed when I got back, down to his shoes, and I pouted internally. I pulled on my jeans and grabbed a sweatshirt and my flip-flops.

I unlatched the window and climbed out first, offering Stefan a hand. But he got through with no trouble, and smiled as he looked around.

I had planted leeks and tomatoes in three large pots that took up most of the fire escape.

"Go on up." I pointed to the iron ladder that led to the roof and he just stared at it. "Unless you're not good with heights?"

"No, it's fine."

It took him a minute, but then he began to climb slowly, that amazing ass taunting me at face level.

Every time I crested the rooftop, I felt the same burst of satisfaction as the first time. My apartment was eclectic and personal. My garden was a more public space. It was where I had coffee in the morning and ate dinner at night. Where I hung out when I had people over, where I waved to neighbors on their fire escapes and the people half a block down who had their own rooftop space.

I stood beside Stefan and watched him take it all in. The low, flat beds of different lettuces and vegetables. The riot of wildflowers along the far perimeter of the rooftop, growing in everything from plastic Trader Joe's bags and galoshes to metal washtubs and holiday popcorn tins. The lavender bushes beside them.

Hardy ice plant, flameflower, and a variety of different stonecrops filled the space between the vegetables and the wildflowers. My Japanese maple grew in the corner behind the windbreak of the taller building next door, in a stack of soil-filled tires like the ones I'd used for Mrs. Portillo's herb garden.

The table and chairs were set up near the tree to take advantage of the same windbreak. I plugged in the white fairy lights since the sun would be setting soon, and heard Stefan's intake of breath.

It looked magical. The transom to our right glowed with lights, and they snaked along the ground. I'd originally set them up for safety purposes, but now I just liked how they looked.

"Hey, you want a beer?" Stefan gaped at me but nodded. "Look around. I'll be right back."

I shimmied down the ladder and grabbed two beers from the fridge, slipping them into my back pockets to scale the ladder again, and found Stefan examining my downspout diverter.

"The rainwater is caught by the gutters, and goes into the downspout. I use the downspout diverter to harvest it and store it in those barrels, then I use it to water everything up here. And if it's really rainy, I just stop diverting it for a while and the downspout delivers it away from the building. Sometimes I use inverted umbrellas on the veggie patches in the summer when there's less rain, and if I run out. In the winter, I don't do as much with it, but I catch the snowmelt the same way."

"This is absolutely amazing," Stefan said. I smiled at him and handed him a beer.

"Wanna sit? Or poke around more, whatever you want. You haven't seen my favorite thing yet, but you probably will soon."

Stefan took another lap of the space, then sat down to drink his beer. "I can't believe this is just yours."

"Well I got permission from my landlord a while back, and I told him I'd share the space. But the other tenants with access haven't been interested so far. Not as convenient if you have to climb up five ladders and are sixty years old I guess."

"I suppose so."

"I'm glad, honestly. I designed it exactly like I wanted, and I redesigned it a lot. Experiment. Wind speed versus growing height, seasonal roof temps, pH factor of the unfiltered rainwater and with different filtration systems. I grew a couple of pineapples that fruited last summer."

I turned to Stefan. He was gazing around him like he was in another world. He didn't say anything. I slid an arm up his thigh and he shivered.

"You alive?"

"I see it now," he said. "I really understand it."

"Rooftop gardening? Awesome! I mean, I get that there're problems, you know. The viability of green space access is a huge factor in gentrification, and the recent uptick in homesteading and urban gardening trends has made—"

"No, not rooftop gardening. You. I understand why they chose you."

"Chose me? Who?"

Stefan ducked his head and clasped his hands on his knee. "For the 30 Under 30 list."

That was not what I was expecting. Months before, I'd ended up on *Time Out NY*'s 30 Under 30 list. They had run photos and bios with the list, but I didn't think it was that big a deal. I'd told my parents about it because it was the sort of thing they liked to trot out if commuters got chatty on long subway rides, or a braggy neighbor needed to be brought down a notch. And I told the BBG because I'd requested the article link to my project page on the website. Other than that, though, no one had ever mentioned it to me. "The... You know about that? Wait, is that...?

Stefan covered his face with his hands and nodded. "Yes. It's why I came. That first day."

I pulled his hands away from his face. He looked mortified. "I had wondered why you came to take a tour when you clearly weren't gonna like it."

He sighed.

"Look, as long as this story doesn't end with 'And then I assassinate you by throwing you off your own rooftop,' just tell me, man."

"I saw you on the list. A friend—a colleague—emailed it to me as a dig. Like, 'If there was going to be a botanist on an over-achiever list I would've thought it'd be you.' I, um...I read your bio and I decided I wanted to see for myself. Why you got picked and..."

"And you didn't," I finished.

I was about to tease him for being so competitive, but even in the fading light of sunset, I could see something was wrong. Stefan didn't just look embarrassed or jealous. He looked ashamed.

"You know that list isn't really about being the best in a field, right? It's about people who are doing projects they can make seem cool or interesting to tourists. They weren't looking to fill a botanist slot so they compared botanists and thought I was better. It's not about merit. It's...clickbait. Something they can link tourists to because they make us sound cool."

Stefan nodded and shrugged again.

"If you know that then why do you care?"

"Because...I guess that's *why* I care. Because I'll never be that person. I've never been that person." He finally met my eyes. "People don't like me," he said simply. "They don't think I'm cool. They never have."

It broke my heart a little bit to hear him say it. More to see how much he clearly believed it. I could give him a pep talk, point out all of his accomplishments. But he already knew those things, and it wasn't what he needed to hear. Instead, I put my hand on his thigh and squeezed.

"I like you."

And damn that smile was fine.

As the sun finally dipped behind the buildings, I heard the first one.

"Look." I pointed at two glowing dots approaching us in the dark.

"What the hell?"

There was a loud meow and then a satisfied purr, and Brutus jumped into my lap.

"Um. Hope you're not allergic." I pointed again, and Stefan and I watched as the nightly parade began.

"There's a drop-off over there," I explained. "Two feet or so. Then another roof. Then another drop. That leads to the loading bay of the building next door, and there's a tree that grows next to it. I planted catnip like a trail leading from the tree, up the loading bay, then leading up here. They come every night."

Stefan's mouth was open.

"This is Brutus. That's what I call him anyway. It's his roof name." I winked. Brutus purred. Stefan stared.

"You...lured cats to your roof with a breadcrumb trail of catnip?" Stefan said.

"I like cats, bro, okay?!"

Stefan's smile was soft. He leaned in slowly, avoiding Brutus, and kissed me.

"Okay."

6

STEFAN

THE SUN HAD LONG since set and my stomach was growling, but I was standing in the doorway to Lab C, staring at the row of plant samples. Usually, even on days when my research was going poorly, or my colleagues were horrible, or a paper I'd submitted got rejected, looking at the living, growing fruits of my labor flooded me with a deep satisfaction.

Proof that I had the ability to change the natural order made me feel powerful. Evidence of my mastery of my subject.

Tonight, though, I didn't feel satisfaction. I didn't really feel anything.

Last weekend, at Milo's, I'd felt...everything. It had been warmth and humor and passion. I had felt alive. When I left to go home, Milo had hugged me. Wrapped his arms around me and squeezed tight, like he actually cared that I was leaving. Then he'd slapped my ass and said goodbye to it too, and I hadn't even minded, because it was proof of what we'd shared.

If walking into Milo's apartment had felt like stepping through a mundane closet to reach a magic world, then re-entering my own world had felt as jarring and disappointing as going back into that closet. Things I'd never given a second thought to—my routine, the calm order of my apartment—seemed flat and dim by comparison.

He'd texted me a few times during the week. A picture of one of his rooftop cats perching on his shoulder with a paw in his curly hair. One of the turtles sunning themselves on the rock near the Japanese garden in the BBG. And one I'd probably stared at a hundred times in the day since he sent it.

It was Milo, sprawled on his bed, shirtless, hair falling into his eyes, light brown skin slightly flushed and sweat-sheened, eyelids half lowered. The image was slightly blurry, like he'd moved the camera as he snapped the picture, and I knew exactly what he was doing with the other hand. I knew that expression. The message just said *More fun w you here* and an emoji of a peach.

The sound of footsteps startled me and I wheeled around.

"You're here late."

Dr. Sorenson was a legend in our field, and a god at Scion. At seventy-six, he still worked five days a week, and published regularly. His suits were impeccable and his white hair gleamed. The rumor was that he wasn't human. Only a replicant could do what Sorenson did. I had worshipped him since graduate school. His was the research I followed obsessively, his the career path I desired for myself. He was my ambition personified, and the day he'd hired me straight out of grad school had been the proudest day of my life.

"Just checking up on a few things, sir."

"Good man." Dr. Sorenson clapped me on the shoulder. "I'm glad to have run into you, Albemarle. Saves me having to write one more email."

"Of course, sir. What can I do for you?"

"It's what you can do for yourself, in fact. Marling is retiring in six months." He said *retiring* like it was a disease. "Rather than hiring an outside man, I'd like to divide his duties among those who have proven themselves dependable. Those with ambition. Those with focus. Like you."

Dr. Sorenson's voice echoed through the empty marble hallway. My ears rang with it.

"I...thank you, sir. I'm honored you think of me that way."

Dr. Sorenson just nodded imperially. "In your case, it would mean taking over his laboratory and interfacing with several of his contacts at pharmaceutical companies. Details, details." He waved as if they were nothing. "Something like ten hours a week more time put in, and a fifteen percent salary bump. More research funding from certain endowments. You know the drill."

I nodded, but wished he would've sent the email after all, because I definitely did not know the drill.

"You'll apply, along with a few others. I'll make my decision based on your plans for the future of your research, and in what direction you believe that takes this company."

He clapped me on the shoulder once more, and turned to walk away, eyes already checking something else on his phone.

"Oh, sir," I called after him. He stopped walking but didn't turn. "When should I have that application to you?"

"End of next week will be fine."

He walked away, leaving me with my mouth hanging open and my eyebrows trying to crawl into my hairline. End of next *week*? It was already Friday night! *Jesus.*

"Okay, I will. Thank you, sir," I called. He waved a careless hand in the air and never stopped walking.

———

A LOUD BUZZING startled me awake, papers spilling off my chest onto the floor, and I nearly fell off the couch with them. Apparently I'd fallen asleep here last night while I tried to get started on my application for Dr. Sorenson.

My phone buzzed again and I grabbed for it. When I saw Milo's name on the texts, I scrambled upright.

I have the day off, wanna help me fill it?, he'd written, and added a leering emoji. Then, *Or we could hang in my garden... supposed to be warm today.* A string of plant and flower and sun emojis followed, and a grinning cat emoji finished the message. I was charmed by how much he liked emojis, as if one language wasn't enough to express himself and he needed to paint a picture with another.

I realized I was smiling widely at Milo's messages. The ellipses that meant he was typing appeared and I was glued to the screen waiting for what he'd say next. But after the dots started and stopped a few times, they disappeared.

Sitting out on Milo's rooftop, looking over the city, maybe holding his hand or kissing him? It sounded wonderful. A repeat of our activities *inside* his apartment...mind-blowing.

But I only had a week to convince Dr. Sorenson that I was the right candidate for this promotion. Seven days to take my career to the next level. I dithered over what to say before I finally responded.

I really wish I could. But I got a rather unexpected opportunity at work yesterday, and I really need to spend all my time seeing it through.

I put my phone facedown on the coffee table and went to shower. But even though the clean, invigorating scent of my soap usually got me in the right headspace to face the day to come, this morning I felt restless. Dissatisfied.

When I picked up my phone, Milo had replied. The photo was of him wrapped in a forest green hooded sweatshirt, holding a cup of steaming coffee. He was pouting, but his eyes still smiled. His dark curls were messier than usual, as if he'd rolled out of bed and gone straight up to the roof. He was so beautiful.

I could see rooftops behind him and the riot of the early wildflowers blooming to his right. Above him was bright blue sky. I glanced out the window and saw that same blue, only it didn't look as good as it did in Milo's picture.

He'd written *I understand. Hope its a good opportunity? Lemme know if you change your mind...*

I sighed and went to make coffee. I'd done the right thing. This job was everything I'd worked for, and now my hard work was being recognized. There was no way I could conscience not giving this application my complete attention. You couldn't just run off and hang out in a garden, making out with a beautiful, sweet, smart man when there was work to be done. That's not how you accomplished anything.

The voice in my head was the one I'd heard for as long as I could remember. It was the voice that had gotten me straight As in high school so that I could get into a good college; gotten me honors in college so I could get into a good grad school. It was the voice that had me triple-check everything I did because carelessness made work for other people, and mistakes showed that you were unprepared.

I listened to the voice because it had gotten me where I was today. I looked around at my immaculate kitchen and my living room as shipshape as a showroom, except for the stack of papers I'd left on the coffee table. I looked around at the diplomas hung over my writing desk, and the accolades I'd collected along the way.

Yes, I listened to the voice because it had gotten me where I was today. But as I glanced over at my phone again, another voice started whispering. This one said *You listened to the voice because you didn't have anything else you wanted to do anyway. Or anyone who wanted to do it with you. You listened to the voice because it was all you knew how to do.*

I straightened my spine and poured a cup of coffee and glared at my phone as if this new voice issued from it.

"Lots to do," I said. "Let's get started."

BY TEN P.M., I'd outlined my plan for my application. Since I didn't know who else Sorenson had tapped for the opportunity, I didn't know what I was competing against, but it seemed logical to cover all my bases, so I'd spent the first half of the day catching up on all the research my colleagues had been working on in the last year. Once I had an idea of where my work was situated with regard to theirs, I knew how to argue for its relevance and its centrality.

Satisfied that I'd cooked up a plan I could execute in a week, I turned to actual cooking. I grabbed my phone to put on a podcast while I cooked and realized I'd never replied to Milo's text from this morning.

There he was, frozen in time, the morning light painting his hair, his garden blooming around him. Damn it, I was smiling again. But the picture also filled me with a kind of melancholy ache. The opportunity for me to share that moment was gone.

It is a good opportunity, thank you, I wrote back. Then, when that seemed unsatisfying: *I hope you had a wonderful day off.*

I hit play on a podcast about architectural design because I didn't want to dwell on what Milo might be doing on a Saturday night. He was so warm, so easygoing—it seemed a given he would have a large group of friends. And probably lovers as well. Certainly the level of...aptitude he displayed in bed last weekend didn't develop without ample experience.

I chopped carrots vigorously, the thought of Milo's bright smile turned on another man making my stomach churn.

But the ding of my phone came almost immediately.

It was p nice. Woulda been better with you tho. Then one single smiley face.

My heart pounded and I stared at the phone with no idea how to respond. Before I could, Milo wrote: *Listen idk how long yr work things gonna take but you should come to the BBG tomorrow and chill w me and the Erasmus kids.*

Then: *I mean, you probably want to check on yr baby anyway, right?* Then a gif of Audrey from *Little Shop of Horrors* captioned "Feed me, Seymour!"

I ignored the horrible movie reference and let that offer rattle around as I chopped broccoli, onion, and cauliflower. Could I afford to take the day off? I had gotten a lot done today... but I'd have to be working on the application on top of all my regular work this week.

After a few minutes, another text came through: *If you want —no presh. Listen if I'm coming on too hard lemme know ok? I can't tell with you.*

This was why I hated texting. The expectation that if you didn't respond immediately it implied some kind of intrinsic disapproval or rejection. But the last part of Milo's message brought me up short. How on earth could he not tell the kind of effect he had on me? He was the first person in years I'd had more than a casual or work-related conversation with!

Yes, but he doesn't know that, the new voice said.

I scrolled up to the picture of Milo again, and made a snap decision.

Okay, I texted back.

I felt a lightness in my chest at the knowledge that I would see Milo tomorrow and realized I was smiling again.

Ok you'll tell me to back my ass off if I'm coming on too strong or ok you wanna hang at BBG tomorrow? Milo responded, with no emojis.

"God dammit, Stefan," I snapped.

That was unclear; I apologize. I meant okay, I'd like to come see you tomorrow.

Yay! Milo responded.

I fiddled with my phone. It felt like there was more to say, but I wasn't sure what. Finally I just wrote, *You're not coming on too strong. I didn't really think of it as coming on at all.*

Yea well. I was gonna say bring yr hot ass over here so I can bury myself in it all night but I went with subtle instead. Then a winky face, another emoji of a peach, and a smiley face with a halo.

A wave of lust washed over me. *Bury myself* expanded to fill my whole field of vision, and I was right back in Milo's bed, with Milo's filthy words in my ear, and his lips on my throat and his gorgeous cock buried so deep it was like he'd be inside me forever.

"*Fuck*," I groaned as I hardened in my pants.

My phone buzzed. *Are you turned on or embarrassed rn?* he wrote. *Or maybe both...*

Both. Absolutely both.

Bc you have nooooothing to be embarrassed about. Just saying.

I wrote back, *All right, see you tomorrow* before I could do anything ridiculous. I went back to chopping vegetables, so that I could eat and get a good night's sleep.

A good night's sleep and a plan for the week. Yes, that was all I needed to get back to feeling like things were under control.

———

I WAS SO glad I'd agreed to come today. I'd agonized over taking the time the whole train ride from Chelsea, but helping the Erasmus students tend to their plants and flowers (and moss smoothies) and plan how they were going to bring growing things into their neighborhoods had flooded me with an exuberant satisfaction, like a huge breath of oxygen-rich air.

The five minutes of making out with Milo before the students showed up hadn't hurt, either.

After the students left, Milo had convinced me to go back to his apartment with him. It hadn't been very difficult, if I was honest. I knew I should spend the evening working on my application, but with one smile and a wicked look in his eyes, Milo had promised me a much better evening.

Now, he was chatting happily as we walked, running through the things he had to do and the people he had to contact to make sure all their neighborhood projects came to fruition. It was an impressive amount of work, and I told him so.

He grinned and bumped my shoulder as we walked.

"Oh, man, the looks on their faces when they see their stuff growing for the first time in their neighborhoods? It's fucking priceless. They're all...I dunno, hopeful? They see this thing that they did—this way they changed something for the better—and you can *see* the moment they realize it's all possible."

"All what?"

Milo looked up at the sky. "Anything. They look at what they created, and the change they made, and they realize that they have the power to change the world. And once you know it...you can't ever un-know it. You know?"

Did I? I had felt it in the lab: the power I had over life itself. The power to change something. To create something. And yet, I wasn't sure I'd ever thought that my power reached beyond the walls of the lab or the pages of the academic journals I published in.

"Oh, so I got the weirdest phone call the other day," Milo said as we reached his building.

"Hmm?"

"This lady from...uh, I forget where, actually. I wrote it down. She saw me in the *Time Out* NY list and wants to put me in this calendar to raise money for a literacy foundation." He shook his head. "I guess kind of like the naked rowers thing?"

"Ah, pardon?"

"You know, those white dudes who pose with paddles in front of their junk? In England?"

71

"It doesn't ring a bell."

Milo opened his front door and even though I was prepared for it this time, it still took my breath away.

"So are you going to do it?"

"I would've said no right away, but I listened to the message while I was at work and Cynthia heard me—she's one of my bosses—and she was saying what good exposure it would be for the BBG..."

"Exposure is right," I muttered.

He shot me a pouty glare that quickly turned predatory.

"I think you need a little bit more exposure right now." He unbuttoned my shirt, put his nose to my neck, and breathed in. "You smell good."

"Mm, so do you." I didn't know how he managed to smell good after spending hours outside, digging in the dirt, but he did. "So you'd do it to help the BBG?"

Milo shrugged, looking shy all of a sudden. "I guess maybe it would be good for future fundraising efforts. I just...it's weird. I don't want to be...naked. In *front* of people?" He crossed his arms and shivered. "And how did they decide who to ask, anyway?"

"From your picture, obviously," I said, and Milo's eyes widened.

"You think I'm cute, Albemarle? You think I should be a calendar model? You want to hang a picture of me on your wall?"

"Yes, no, yes—I mean, no. I mean. I forgot the order of the questions."

I couldn't really pay attention to anything with Milo's gorgeous mouth this close to mine and his talented hand working me through my pants.

"How do they know I don't have some kind of horribly offensive tattoo that takes up my whole chest or something?" he murmured, lips grazing my chin. "Or...or—"

I kissed him and his words dissolved into the heat of our mouths moving together. He stroked me just right and I groaned and sucked on his tongue.

"Getmoff," Milo said, yanking at my pants. "I want you. I wanna fuck you. Please, can I, please?"

He was pure, heady desire, hands and mouth everywhere. No one had ever wanted me like this. No one had ever made me feel anything like this. "Yes, please," I gasped.

"So fucking polite."

He pushed me onto the low bed and stripped my clothes off, never breaking eye contact. The look of hunger in his eyes made me so hard I was panting by the time he got his own clothes off.

"Lemme see it," he growled. I turned over onto my stomach and his hands were on my ass within a second. "Mmmm, hello," he said. And before I could mention the fact that he'd just greeted my ass, he spread me open and licked me until I was writhing on the bed.

"Oh, Jesus, I want you, fuck." I was chanting nonsense into the pillow and Milo was dragging his leaking erection against my thigh.

"Yes, fuck, I don't wanna go slow this time. Okay?"

I nodded. I didn't want slow. I didn't want time to think, or reflect, or wonder, or worry. I wanted to feel Milo and only Milo, everywhere.

There was a rip, then a flick, and then Milo's hard, slippery cock prodded my entrance.

"Yeah?" he asked, licking up the back of my neck. I nodded again and he penetrated me in one deep, plowing thrust.

I shouted and grabbed at the pillow, and Milo whimpered, hands sweet on my back and over my ribs until I relaxed. Then he started to move and it was hard and fast and perfect. I couldn't think, couldn't speak. I just held on, rocking back to meet Milo's thrusts with my own.

"Shit, yes, fuck yourself on my dick. So fucking hot like this." Milo growled and bit my neck.

Every inch of my skin was vibrating. My cock was so hard it was dripping into the bedclothes, and each time Milo slid inside me, a pleasure so deep it was almost pain rocked me. I felt like I was coming apart and the instrument of my demise was the only thing I was living for.

"Please," I heard someone say over and over, and I only realized it was me when Milo groaned and said, "I got you, babe. I want you to come all over my bed so I can smell you the next time I jerk off. Imagine I'm still inside this tight ass. Pretend I'm just fucking you forever and ever, and—"

I screamed when his rough hand slid up my erection, the pressure so exquisite I lost track of my body in space. The next thing I knew, I had collapsed flat on my stomach. My cock was trapped between the bed and Milo's hand, and I thrust into the tunnel they made, every nerve ending on fire.

Milo was talking a constant stream of the hottest filth I'd ever heard and I could only half hear it because my ears were ringing.

"Come for me, baby. Come with me deep in here, I wanna feel your ass clamp down on my dick like you're sucking me inside. So good, babe, you feel so fucking good, wanna stay in here forever..."

The pleasure was climbing higher and higher and I had been on the edge for so long. I tilted my hips up a little so he was striking my prostate with every stroke, and when his hand pressed my cock into the bed, I was gone, coming in heaving pulses that tensed every muscle.

Milo stroked me through it, groaning in my ear as I tightened around him again and again. His rhythm stuttered, and as the last shuddery fingers of pleasure left me gasping on the bed, he drove himself deep inside me and shouted out his orgasm. Each stroke was exquisite torture, I was so sensitive, and by the time Milo finally came down, pressing kisses along my shoulder, I was shaking. A nip to my neck sent a shiver of pleasure through my overstimulated body and I clenched around him involuntarily.

"Ohhh, fuck," he moaned, pressing his hips against me and shuddering. "Okay, Jesus."

He stayed inside me for a minute as our breathing slowed, and when he pulled out gently and I rolled over, his eyes were sleepy and bright, and his cheeks and neck were flushed. I looked down to find myself, yet again, covered in come.

"Mmmm," Milo said, and with a wicked wink, he bent down and licked a slow swipe over the head of my cock. I was so sensitive it felt like sandpaper, and I pushed him away even as my stupid penis tried to get hard again.

"Stop, stop, you'll kill me," I said. Milo grinned and kissed my thigh instead.

I knew I should get up, get dressed, go home, work on my application. But Milo slipped a hand behind my neck and kissed me so sweet I couldn't do anything but kiss him back. I smiled against his mouth and I could feel him smiling too. Then my stomach gave a loud growl and my eyes flew open.

"Well, I really enjoy killing you like this—" Milo's hand closed around my cock again, and I jerked away, groaning. "But I don't want to actually watch you expire from starvation. Want some eggs?"

Well...I would have to eat, right?

"Okay, thanks."

I reached for my shirt and Milo pressed me back down with a hand on my chest. "You just stay there all naked and gorgeous. I got it."

He padded away, still naked himself, and I let my eyes close at the sound of him moving around in the kitchen. He hummed as he cooked, and it made me smile. Sprawled on my back in his warm bed, with the trailing tendril of the fiddle-leaf fig hovering overhead like a sentinel, I had never felt more content. I let my eyes drift almost shut so that green filled my whole vision and I imagined Milo doing that as he lay here.

What was it like to wake up in this apartment, life blooming all around? I must've fallen asleep because the next thing I knew, Milo was sauntering back in and offering me a bowl. "Here you go."

He settled back in beside me, cross-legged, seeming so totally at ease in his nudity that I wondered at the shyness he'd expressed about the calendar shoot.

"Thank you." I took a bite of the creamy eggs and sighed. "These are really good. Thanks." He smiled and we ate quietly for a few minutes.

"Hey, what was your work thing?" he asked, and all the ease left me, the moment popping like a balloon. "Or we don't have to talk about it," Milo said, eyes on me.

"Oh, no, it's good. The timeline's just a little tight." I finished the last bite of egg and put the bowl on the nightstand. "One of the senior botanists in my lab is retiring, and my boss invited me to apply to take over a portion of his responsibilities. It's a big honor, really, that he asked me." I sat up straighter. "It would mean more funding directed at my research, and more control over the direction of the lab in general—its collaborations, acquisitions, et cetera. It would mean longer hours, of course, but it also comes with substantial compensation. *If* I get it, that is."

Milo raised an eyebrow. "You like being in control?" he asked.

"I— Yes." He raised an eyebrow and I felt my cheeks heat. "At work, I do. In my life. Anyway, I need to get a comprehensive application that outlines my vision for the work—and my qualifications, of course—to my boss by the end of the week, so..."

I trailed off as I slid back into planning mode, mentally reallocating the hours of my week to make as much time as possible to work on the application.

Milo smiled but his brow was furrowed. "Congrats on getting asked," he said. "They must think you're great."

He paused and then started shoving the rest of his eggs in his mouth. Clearly there was something he wasn't saying.

"But?" I asked.

He slid his bowl next to mine and squinted at me.

"But...well, last weekend you were talking about how busy you've been lately, and how you were happy that you'd come to the BBG. And you worked all day yesterday, and just fell asleep when I was gone for five minutes. It just sounds like you'd be even busier, doing more of what you're already doing."

He put a warm hand on my thigh and I went rigid under his touch.

"Which isn't bad," he said. "If that's what you want. It just seems like...you know what, never mind. Sorry. It's not my place."

"No, say it. Say what you were going to say."

He shook his head but after a moment he leaned closer to me. His expression was pitying, and my heart started to race.

"Babe, you just...fuck, it's just...there's so much *more* to you than this job. And I don't think you even know."

My spine straightened and I pulled my shoulders back. "Look, you've made it very clear that you don't approve of my job."

"I never said that."

"You didn't have to say it. You just had to say 'Plant eugenics' and you made it very clear that you think I'm not better than some asshole trying make a buck on genetically modified novelty roses."

"Well what is it about your job that you feel most strongly about? What part of it is most important to you?"

His tone was sincere, and so was his expression. He really

wanted to know, and I...I really wanted to shove him away and run.

Obviously my work was important! I worked at one of the top labs in the country! We were constantly discovering new botanical properties that could be used in medicines and environmental applications, and that was just the beginning!

"Listen," Milo said, stopping my racing thoughts, "I'm not trying to be a dick. It's your work, and of course it's important to you. You don't have to explain yourself to me. All I'm saying is that sometimes we pay so much attention to the fact that we have the chance for *more* of something that we don't stop to ask ourselves if it's a thing we actually *want* more of. More isn't always better. Sometimes more of one thing is just less you can have of everything else."

I pushed myself out of bed and started pulling my clothes back on.

"Stefan, come on. Please don't go."

I shook my head and concentrated on putting my shirt on right-side out. "I need to get home. I have work to do on my application for my useless job."

He stood too, palms up, quelling. "I'm sure your job's not useless! Don't put words in my mouth. Just wait. I'm sorry I hurt your feelings. I only meant there are so many things you could do. You have so much energy and passion and love..." He trailed off at my expression.

I was vibrating with hurt and anger. He looked at me and saw wasted potential instead of achievement...it was almost more than I could bear. "That's incredibly insulting. And patronizing," I said, stepping into my shoes. "Excuse me."

I spun around and made for the door, clinging to the one positive thought I had, which was that I had timed things well enough that I could leave having gotten the last word.

Then I found myself pressed against the inside of the door by the weight of Milo's body.

"Hey," he said fiercely. "I'm sorry. I didn't mean to insult you or patronize you. I didn't mean to dismiss your job, but I see that I did, and I apologize." He cupped my cheek. "But please believe that I meant it when I said that I see so much in you that you keep locked inside. Inside, you're like...like heat and passion and... Fuck, I don't know what I'm trying to say. I just don't get why you'd want to trap all that in ten extra hours of work a week instead of—"

"Instead of coming here and fucking you?" I snapped.

His eyes narrowed. "Well, I'll tell you what, babe. Every time you talk about work, even when you say good things, your shoulders are tense and you look distracted. When I'm fucking you, you writhe underneath me in total abandon. You're relaxed and free and you say my name like you're talking to god. So I think you could probably do worse."

His eyes were heated and he was speaking in that filthy voice he used while we were in bed, and he was so close that every inhale brought his chest to mine. He was self-righteous and cocky and infuriating. And somehow I wanted him to make me feel everything he'd just described all over again.

How did I end up here? I'd thought I'd finally found someone who understood me. Who saw me. Who...who liked me.

But he'd turned out to be just like everyone else. He thought I was a pretentious asshole. He thought my work was meaningless. He wanted the version of me he'd decided would be better. He didn't want *me*. He didn't want me at all.

"Fuck you," I spat. Then I pushed him away, and flung open the door so that he wouldn't see me cry.

7

MILO

"I THINK I FUCKED UP," I told Mariana, thunking the back of my head against the wall. Mariana was my sister-in law and she was so awesome I still didn't quite understand how my brother Ricardo had convinced her to marry him. It was lucky for me he had, though, because in the five years since they'd gotten together, she'd become one of my best friends.

"What'd you do now, idiot?" she asked, twisting a long curl of dark hair around her finger and sipping her tequila shot like it was whiskey. "Plant that flower that smells like dead bodies in a nursery school playground or what?"

"I never should've let you read that book about poisonous plants."

"Boy, the day you *let* me do anything is the day I plant flowers on your grave."

I snorted and finished my beer, signaling the waiter for another round. We were sitting at a table outside the bar even though it was a little chilly. Mariana got claustrophobic and I would never choose to be inside if I could be outside, so we were a good match.

It had been beautiful out this week, the full flush of spring bringing everyone outside, eager to drink in the sun. It was why my tours had been so full on Saturday that I hadn't had time to greet everyone individually before we began. In my afternoon tour, there had been a moment when I'd caught a glimpse of a man in the back of the group dressed uncommonly well, in a lilac button-down and a maroon cable-knit sweater, and my heart had leapt.

In the moment I'd thought it was Stefan, I'd lost track of what I was saying, imagining how I'd press him against the first vertical surface I could find and kiss him until he agreed to talk to me again. When the man had stepped to the side and I'd seen it was a stranger, my stomach had dropped, the disappointment sharp and sudden.

"I, uh. I met someone," I said, keeping my voice casual.

"Like, *met* someone or met *someone*?" she asked, performing a subtle grind at the beginning of her sentence and deep eye contact at the end. "Whoa. Met *someone*. I didn't really know you did that?"

I shrugged. Mostly I didn't. Mostly I kept it casual. Sometimes I met people and hooked up; sometimes I fooled around with friends who were into it. With strangers, it was for fun—a release. With friends, I liked giving them something they enjoyed. Either way, it was just sex, just closeness. I wasn't really interested in taking something fun and hot and weighing it down with expectations.

Expectations meant disappointment, and I didn't like to disappoint people.

I'd learned that lesson my first year in grad school, when I met Diego. It was the first day of our orientation, and we were the only two Latinx folks in our cohort. The professor leading the orientation said some foolish thing and our mutual snorts led to knowing eye contact. As everyone drifted out of the room, we left together. He was brilliant and funny and did this thing with his tongue when he was going down on me that made me see stars.

He'd told me he loved me soon after winter break, and I was blindsided. He'd thought we were on a relationship escalator, stair-stepping our way to a knowable future, and I'd been enjoying the bonus of getting to have hot sex with a guy I really enjoyed hanging out with. I tried to explain how wonderful I thought he was but that I just didn't see him that way, and the hurt and disappointment on his face were crushing. I'd never wanted to feel that way again.

There had been hurt and disappointment on Stefan's face the other night, too. And it had filled me with that same sick feeling in the pit of my stomach—the care and pleasure I'd wanted to bring transformed into pain.

The difference was that with Stefan, I had already begun to feel more. To feel different. He didn't feel like a friend I wanted to sleep with, or a hookup I wanted to hang out with. He felt... brighter than everything else around him. Shinier. Everything he did caught my attention; everything he said mattered to me, even when it mattered because I thought he was dead wrong. I *liked* the idea of arguing with him, debating about this or that until our irritation flared into passion and I tumbled him down on my bed and clashed in a very different way.

And, more surprisingly, I liked the idea of waking up next to him. Seeing how the leaf-filtered sunlight changed the planes of his face. Learning how he'd smell if he used my soap and my deodorant after. Knowing with muscle memory the feel of his body in the half-asleep dark.

Shit, I was in some kind of trouble.

I sighed and swallowed down the flutter in my stomach. I filled Mariana in on our initial meeting on the tour and how Stefan had apologized and turned out to be so different than he'd seemed that first day. How much I liked him. Everything I said sounded silly, though, because I was still stuck in the fantasy of waking in the middle of the night to feel Stefan against me, pulling his gorgeous body close, and sinking deep inside him, pulling soft cries out of him as I brought him to clenching climax before he could sort dream from reality.

"He's like this super hot...what's the grown-up version of preppy?"

"Uh, white?"

I laughed. "He's black. But you know what I mean? Like, fancy but not suits?"

She held her shot like it was a teacup, pinkie out. "Business casual?" she offered in a terrible British accent.

"No, like—well, maybe, I dunno. He looks like a magazine ad for a watch you can wear in the mountains or something. Like, all buttoned-up with sweaters and layers and overcoats and more than one pair of glasses kind of hot."

She laughed and shook her head. "Whatever you say, bro."

"Anyway, my point is that he's totally different underneath. Like, he goes from proper and controlled to...uh." I stopped myself from describing the way Stefan shed his control when he shed his clothes, opening up for me like a night-blooming flower.

Mariana narrowed her eyes like she got the picture anyway. "Okay, but you get that *everyone* is more than they seem, yes? Like, you did attend puberty, right? First impressions aren't accurate. Just because someone likes to tuck in their shirt every once in a goddamn while doesn't mean they're a corporate over-lord. Sometimes people like shit in bed that you couldn't guess by looking at them, et cetera? Because if you didn't learn that at thirteen, I'm concerned for you. And, frankly, the world."

"Haha, yes, of course I know that." She raised an eyebrow. "The thing is...he got invited to apply for this promotion at work. Well, it doesn't sound like a promotion to me. It sounds like his boss is willing to up his salary to do more of what he's already doing, but whatever."

"That is literally what most promotions are, yes, continue."

"But that's the thing, he's miserable. He's like...suffocating in his own life. He barely even *has* a life. And if he takes this promotion, he'll just have less time to do anything else and—"

"Stop. You didn't *tell* him that, did you?"

"Well. Yeah."

Mariana shook her head at me, jaw set. "You're so stupid, I can't believe you."

"What? No, come on. I just—"

"No, no, no, for real. How long have you known this guy? Like seven minutes? And what percentage of that did you spend fucking? Like fifty percent? You don't know this guy. You don't know his hopes and dreams. Milo! Come on. And then he tells you this opportunity came up and you decided to lecture him on how he's not living as his full self. What are you, his damn life coach? Get out of here."

She shoved my shoulder in disgust and I swallowed hard. "So, what—I should've smiled and nodded when he clearly hasn't thought it all through? He was so happy to get his boss's approval that he didn't even consider if he wanted the actual life that went with the opportunity."

"Oh, and you know this because you asked him?"

"I—"

"That was rhetorical, asshole. I know you didn't ask him. When you think you know what someone needs, you don't ask them shit. You just tell them." She put a hand on my shoulder. "Look. I love you. But you're a fucking idiot sometimes. You've got to be okay with other people making choices that aren't the same as the choices you would make and not making them feel like crap for it."

Was that what I did? Was I really as much of a judgmental dick as Mariana was saying? It wasn't that I wanted Stefan to make the choice I would make. It was... God, the *look* on his face when he was talking plants with the kids at BBG. He'd looked light and happy. And when he was in my apartment, he'd seemed so free. But every time he mentioned his job he coiled like a spring. And the way he described his routine. Just him and grilled chicken breast and the newest issue of *American Journal of Botany*. It was awful.

"I just can't stand to see people I care about be unhappy," I said finally. "It hurts. To watch them suffer. I just...I hate it."

Mariana's expression softened. "People aren't like plants, you know? You can't just move them around so you can give them more sun, or re-pot them if you think they need more space."

But...weren't they? Didn't we all need to be pointed in the direction of more sun sometimes? Wouldn't most of us like to have enough room to spread our branches and grow our roots?

I'd told Stefan about how I watered the marigolds Mrs. Portillo's husband gave her and how happy it had made me to give her something beautiful. What I hadn't told him was that Mr. Portillo got sick a few months after he brought them home and died the next year. I'd tended those marigolds so avidly because they were a piece of him that I could keep alive for her. And I'd planted flowers and herbs for her ever since, because they were something she could take care of; something she could watch bloom every spring, and bring indoors every winter. It had made her feel better, and that had made me feel good.

But you didn't make Stefan feel better, you made him feel worse.

"I swear," Mariana said. "You and your brother and your dad are all like this."

"What? No way. I'm nothing like Ricky and Dad."

She snorted. "You are. All of you think that your way is the best way and if people don't see it then you try to convince them. Ricardo and your dad gave you hell for going to grad school instead of being a firefighter. Then once you finished, they thought you were nuts to work at the BBG instead of getting a job that paid a bunch of money. You hated when they told you what you should do because you didn't want the same things as them. Now you're doing that same thing to this Stefan guy."

I opened my mouth to argue but she waved me off.

"Whatever, Milo. You think it's different because you're doing it for his own good. But what the hell do you think Ricardo and your dad thought they were doing? You think you know better than him. You think you know how he should spend his time. What does that sound like to you?"

I took a deep breath and pushed down my anger. Mariana's straight-shooting might be painful to hear, but she sure as hell was usually right on target. I ran through her words in my head again.

I *had* thought I knew better than Stefan. I *did* think he was making the wrong choice. And I *hadn't* asked him how he felt about it. Not really.

"It sounds like a complete fucking asshole," I said finally.

Mariana tossed back the rest of her shot. "Bingo."

I TEXTED Stefan as soon as Mariana and I parted ways.

I'm really sorry about the other day. I should never have said that shit to you about your job and it was pointed out to me that I acted like a total dick. Can we talk? I was gonna bring you fancy flowers at work but...yeah that's a terrible idea. Lemme know?

Stefan wrote back hours later: *I appreciate the apology. I'm quite busy at the moment, so it's not convenient.*

Somehow, his icy politeness hurt more than when he'd sworn at me as he left my apartment. At least that had passion, heat. This was Stefan putting me at a distance, as if I had no place in his life.

And I guess I didn't really. I didn't know where he lived. I knew where he worked, but no way was I gonna go all John Cusack with a boom box at his workplace. I just had to hope he'd change his mind.

I really, really hated waiting.

8

STEFAN

TWO WEEKS after I turned in my application to Dr. Sorenson was my mother's birthday. I was heading uptown, dreading the evening, when I got a text from Milo. Just seeing his name was enough to make me swipe my phone so fast I nearly fumbled the gift I was holding.

Milo had texted me so many times since the night we fought. I'd put him off at first, and buried myself in work. But once I'd turned in my application and the texts had kept coming, I'd forced myself to look back over them.

There were sweet texts and apologetic ones, self-deprecating texts and flirtatious ones. Then there were the filthy ones.

At first, I'd tried to convince myself that the only reason I'd come to care so much about Milo so quickly was the way he'd made me feel in bed. The way he'd somehow opened me up and climbed inside me. The way he'd brought me to heights of pleasure I'd never experienced, or even imagined. And that wasn't nothing.

But after every filthy text about what he wanted to do to me, if I'd let him, was a text that said something like: *Fell asleep half off the bed and woke up with a fern in my mouth.* Or: *Planted some* Allium giganteum *on the roof. They kinda remind me of you cuz their stems are so serious but their blooms are wild. Or, once: Morning. If you were a fence and I was a moss smoothie I'd wanna grow all over you. Or vice versa. Whatever yr into ;)*

I had laughed aloud at that one and it had ignited a dull ache in my stomach at the realization that the Erasmus students' plants were growing and I was missing it. That their projects would be moving into their neighborhoods soon and I wouldn't be there to see their faces, the way Milo had told me I should.

Why, then, hadn't I written him back after the first text? Why had I read each message a dozen times, then put my phone down every time without responding?

No matter how sweet his messages, his words the night I told him about my potential promotion had cut deep. I didn't want to deal with how disappointed I was that he'd turned out not to understand me any better than anyone else in my life had. And I was scared that if I spent more time with him, he'd just disappoint me again.

After all, most other people had.

Now, his text said, *Sooo I caved and agreed to this wackadoo photo shoot. Lady in charge finally promised they'd put a bunch of links to my projects and BBG on the website and in the calendar. She probably thinks I'm such a PITA *laughing crying emoji* *angel emoji* Just FYI it's at the BKN lib next Sat at noon...in case you wanted me to make a big scene and say sorry to you in front of a buncha strangers. Naked. In a library. Naked.*

Then: *Or in case you just want to see me make an ass of myself.*

Finally: *Again.*

When I caught a glimpse of my reflection in the train doors two stops later, I was smiling.

THE PARTY WAS AT MY PARENTS' Sugar Hill house, as it

was every year, and like every year, I floated from group to group, picking at the food and wishing I were elsewhere.

"Happy birthday, Mama," I said when I finally found her. I kissed her cheek, breathing in the familiar scent of Arpège, which she'd worn for as long as I could remember.

"Thank you, dear," my mother said. "You look well. Have you brought anyone with you?"

"You know I would have informed you if I was bringing a guest." My voice was sharper than I'd intended. She asked the same thing every time I saw her.

"Of course." She smiled coolly, and slid her arm through mine. It was a possessive, controlling gesture, but I got a flash of when Milo had looped his elbow through mine and tugged us close together. It hadn't felt possessive or controlling when he did it. It had felt excited and intimate.

"Come tell your cousin why she simply must apply to a PhD program in anthropology next year, won't you? She's being ridiculous." But it was a rhetorical question, because she had already maneuvered us over to my aunt Nina and my cousin, Charlotte.

"Oh, Stefan, good," Aunt Nina said, giving me a pat on the shoulder. "Charlotte, let Stefan tell you what graduate school is like. I'm sure he can explain how valuable it is."

My mother and Aunt Nina looked at me with identical expressions of calm superiority. Charlotte sulked between them. She was smart and funny, and my aunt acted like she was constantly on the verge of making a terrible decision.

"You're going to be a senior this coming year, right?"

"Yeah," she said. "And I've been loving my anthro classes. But..." She shrugged. "A PhD is a huge commitment and a lot of time. And I'm not even sure that I want to—"

"Anything worth doing is worth making a commitment to," Aunt Nina said. "And you need an advanced degree. What can you do with a bachelor's degree these days?"

Charlotte's jaw tightened and her fists clenched. "I just think I'm more interested in going to some of the places I've studied, trying to work with people in a more hands-on way."

I nodded. "In the social sciences, a PhD is required if Charlotte wants to be a professor. But if she doesn't, a PhD isn't necessarily very useful."

"But surely a PhD wouldn't *prevent* her from *helping* people," Aunt Nina said with forced cheer. Charlotte and I exchanged looks.

"Well, no, of course not," I said. "But it is a matter of committing to a very rigorous program that can take seven, eight, nine years, with no guarantee of a teaching position on the other side. If Charlotte knows she wants that kind of job, then all that time and effort might be worth it. But if she's more interested in other paths, it's just a lot of work in order to get a degree that won't really serve her."

My mother's lips were pursed in a way that meant trouble, and Aunt Nina had one brow raised. Charlotte's eyes had widened at the words "nine years" and stayed that way.

"Would you all excuse me?" I said. "I need to say hello to Mr. and Mrs. Taylor."

I turned around before they could say anything and walked toward the Taylors. But after saying hello, I snuck up the back staircase and eased inside the quiet time capsule of my old bedroom.

My mother had turned it into a guest room, but it still looked nearly the same as it had when I was in high school, because I'd never put much on the walls. There was the large print of Edward Step's *China Asters* chromolithograph that I'd bought at the Natural History Museum my freshman year, and the framed Köhler poster of *Arachis hypogaea* I'd bought the next year to go with it.

Lying on my back on the bed, the images were so familiar I could almost believe I was a teenager again, reading alone on yet another Saturday night, or watching a movie on my computer as the neighborhood pulsed with activity just outside my open window.

I'd wanted a minute to think, because my words to Charlotte and my aunt had shaken something loose. Something important.

What I'd told them about grad school was similar to what Milo had told me about my promotion, only I hadn't been able to hear it when he'd said it.

He hadn't meant that my promotion was useless, had he? He'd meant that I'd gotten so caught up in the honor of being considered and the pride that would attend being chosen, that I hadn't stopped to assess my goals and then determine if this move would serve them. He hadn't meant I shouldn't apply; he'd meant I should weigh the pros and cons. And he was probably right.

It had become habit to always push for more. More funding, more power, more recognition. Yet the things that had made me feel so alive lately weren't about more of any of those.

More responsibility meant less flexibility to do my own research, which was the part of my job I loved the most, and the reason I'd pursued botany in the first place.

More time spent at work meant less time to help the Erasmus students plant up their neighborhoods, didn't it? And... it meant less time that I could be with Milo, too. Less opportunity to pursue *anything* outside work.

I lay on my childhood bed and stared at the posters I'd stared at so often as a teenager when those habits took root. When I buried myself in schoolwork to take my mind off the fact that I hadn't been invited to a classmate's birthday party. When I studied hours and hours for a test I already knew I could ace because getting the *highest* grade in the class would mean that I was the best at something, even if no one in that class wanted to eat lunch with me.

I'd run toward more for so long that I'd forgotten what I was running from. Loneliness. Hurt. Fear.

I stared at the posters for so long the colors blurred. Lying here would be better with Milo beside me, probably squirming for more territory on the twin bed. This party would be better with Milo beside me. I could imagine him telling my mother what he did with that crooked grin. Not "I'm a botanist in charge of Outreach and Programming at the Brooklyn Botanic Garden," but "I plant stuff, and help kids plant stuff."

Everything would be better with Milo beside you. It felt like the clearest thought I'd had in years.

9

MILO

I WAS GOING TO PUKE. I was going to puke in the street in front of the crowds at Grand Army Plaza Greenmarket, and that would *still* be less embarrassing than what I was about to do. What on earth had I been thinking when I agreed to this?

I skirted the edges of the market and sat on a step of the library, head between my knees, swearing at myself rabidly. Maybe it wasn't too late. Maybe I could just go in and tell them, "Hey, sorry to waste your time, but even if it is for charity, and even if it is great exposure for the BBG, I would rather not expose *myself* to a bunch of strangers.

"Oh my god, this is the worst idea I've ever had," I groaned into my hands.

No, actually, being a dick to Stefan was the worst idea you ever had because you haven't felt like that about anyone ever, and you scared him away forever. Also: DICK.

"Uh, Milo?"

I jerked my head out of my hands and looked up into the anxious face of Stefan Albemarle. My heart slammed against my ribcage and I blinked to make sure I wasn't having some kind of nerves-induced hallucination.

"Hi! Hello, hi. Shit, hi, Stefan." I stood up so he wasn't

towering over me and wobbled on my feet. Stefan reached out a hand and caught my shoulder and all I wanted at that moment was to pull him into my arms.

"Please can I kiss you?" is what came out of my mouth when I started to say another nervous *Hi*.

Stefan's eyes went wide.

"Sorry, Jesus. Please attribute everything stupid I say to the fact that I am freaking out right now. Also, hi. It's really fucking good to see you."

His smile was small, but it was there and it was genuine and it meant there was hope. Hope that I hadn't screwed up this thing between us forever.

"Listen, please can we go somewhere and talk? So I can apologize for real?" I slid my hands onto his shoulders and almost groaned when his eyes fluttered shut for a moment. "I was a total dick, man. I know I was. I was patronizing and, and all the other things you said, but if you'll let me apologize—"

"Stop, stop. Later, okay? Now you have to get inside or you're going to be late." He looked at his watch to underscore the point.

"I don't fucking care about being late. I wanna talk to you."

"Being late is rude and disrespectful," Stefan said primly.

And I smiled so big it almost hurt. It was such a perfectly Stefan thing to say. "Okay, but seriously, this was a huge mistake. I don't want to take my clothes off in front of people. It's creepy and weird. Can't we just go? Look, the farmers market!"

"No, no, absolutely not."

Stefan took me by the arm, walked me up the steps, and leaned against the wall beside the bronze gateway. He looked around as if to check if anyone was paying attention and then he cleared his throat nervously. "You didn't seem shy taking your clothes off before."

The heat in his voice inspired an answering heat in my groin and I tugged him close. If he was going to push me away, so be it, but I wasn't going to let the chance go by without trying.

"Because that was just for you," I said in his ear. I relished the shiver that ran through him and closed the distance between us, kissing him softly beneath his ear.

He gasped and pulled away.

"I, um...I brought some stuff for you. For the photo shoot. It probably wasn't my place, but..." He shook his head and took my hand. His was shaking. "I have thought of you so often. And the other day, I— Well, we can talk later. But I wanted to come here and see you and say...yes, let's talk."

My relief was overwhelming and I pulled Stefan close and hugged him to me. "Thank you."

He nodded. "So, do you want to see what I brought? If you really don't want to do the shoot, of course you don't have to."

With him next to me, it suddenly felt like much less of a big deal. "Yeah, okay. Let's see."

We went inside through the entrance hall and took the stairs to the second floor. I followed Stefan to a closed reading room. There was a photographer with an intimidatingly professional camera and lighting setup, and a few people milling around.

"Oh hey, Stefan. This Milo?" someone was saying, but I didn't notice anyone or anything except the plants.

In front of the bookshelves, and on the bookshelves, and leaning against the bookshelves, were dozens of plants. There were orchids and bonsai, ivies and marigolds. On the wooden chair sat a gorgeous *Mimosa pudica*. It was all the plants Stefan and I had talked about since the first day we met.

"Oh my god," I said, turning to him. He ducked his head, but not before I saw how pleased he looked. "Stefan, this is...this is amazing. But you do get that I'm supposed to be apologizing to *you*, right? I'm the one who needs a grand gesture."

"It's not an apology," he said. "You make things happen for so many other people. You arrange things behind the scenes, and do a huge amount of work so that they can see their vision come to life. I just wanted to set a scene that would reflect who you are."

My throat tightened and my ears prickled. I slid a hand around the back of his neck and drew his mouth to mine. I kissed him softly, gently, just a press of lips, but I thought he could feel how much I meant by it.

"There's one more thing." He slid a book off the chair and handed it to me.

It was *A Tree Grows in Brooklyn*, the novel I'd read the cover off of when I'd found it at a book stall in the park the same summer I'd discovered the world of plants.

"It seemed apt," Stefan said. "There was a 1943 edition, but it was for in-library use only. Besides, it was just a clothbound cover so you couldn't see the title well. I thought this was much more graphic for the purposes of the camera, but—"

"Shut up, it's amazing." *You're amazing.* The thought sprang to my mind so immediately that for a moment I wasn't sure if I'd accidentally said it out loud. "Thank you. It's perfect."

Stefan smiled and looked down.

"Milo, I assume?" The woman with the camera held out her hand. "I'm Van. I'll be doing your shoot today."

She was tall and striking, with flawless dark skin, short, natural hair bleached platinum, and lines of gold rings piercing both ears from lobe to helix. Her black jeans slouched into white high-tops, and her worn black T-shirt showed the swooping tattoos that covered her arms and chest. She was stunning.

"Hey," I said. "Um, you basically look so cool that suddenly I feel like maybe you could make me look cool in these pictures."

She saluted me with the camera. "I'll see what I can do. I'm not a miracle worker." She gave me a lazy smirk to show she was kidding and I liked her immediately.

I was bustled into hair and makeup and someone worked

gunk into my curls while Van and her assistant explained how the shoot would go. They loved the plants Stefan had brought in and they'd pulled all the green books on the shelves out to maximize their color.

The makeup artist's gaze swept over my worn jeans, T-shirt, and work boots. "I can just make it look like you're not wearing any makeup," he said. "Just even out your skin a little and highlight your cheekbones. Or..." He looked over at the set and raised a perfectly arched brow. "I *could* do something a little more interesting."

It was unnerving being examined like a specimen. "Like?"

"Like, I could do your makeup in a subtle green palette. Make you look kinda...plant-ish. Just a slightly green highlight on your cheekbones, a dark green eyeliner. It'd be cool. Your choice, though."

He shrugged like he thought I wouldn't go for it. I'd never worn makeup before, period. But here I was, doing this ridiculous thing, and Stefan had gone to all this trouble to make it awesome. I might as well go all out, right?

"Yeah, cool, man, do the green thing."

His eyes lit up. "Yeah? *Awesome.* It's gonna be great, I promise."

True to his word, thirty minutes later—and one hundred percent more naked—I looked in the mirror and looking back at me was a stranger. Dark curls spiraled around his face, and his cheekbones and jaw looked sharp and defined while his eyes looked dreamy. He was...almost ethereal. But Dale—I'd learned as he worked—had managed to make it look cool, like a supervillain or something.

"I look..." I shook my head. "Thanks, man."

"You look beautiful."

Stefan had hung back since things had gotten started, but now he was looking down at me with wide eyes.

"You do," Dale said. "A vast improvement." He winked and left me to Stefan.

"This whole crew the snark parade, or what?"

Stefan didn't answer. His eyes trailed over my painted face and the green-tinted shimmer that accentuated my collarbones and hip bones and shadowed my lean muscles to exaggerate their lines.

I was wearing what Van had called a cock sock, to hide my junk, but other than that I was naked beneath my loosely tied robe.

But now that I was essentially in a costume of hair and makeup, I didn't feel quite so exposed. It wasn't really going to be me in these photographs, it was this otherworldly plant creature. I kinda liked it.

"You're gonna stay, right?"

"I'd like to," Stefan said, eyes still on my shimmery nipples. I covered my chest with my hands in mock modesty and Stefan finally made eye contact. "If that's okay."

I nodded, feeling all hot and fidgety from the way he was looking at me. "I really wanna kiss you right now," I grumbled. "But it'd mess up my makeup."

"We're all set," Van said. "Let's get started."

Stefan shot me a heated look as I slid off my robe and handed it to him. Suddenly my heart was pounding again and I was extremely glad that Dale and Rose, the hairstylist, were waiting outside during the shoot.

Van posed me among the plants and books, arranging a branch here and a tendril there. She had me pose with *A Tree Grows In Brooklyn* covering my junk in some of them, and in others she had me reading the book while the plants covered me. She told me what to do with my face and to move my hand an inch in that direction or my knee five degrees in the other direction until I felt like I was playing Twister.

"Being a model isn't as glamorous as I imagined," I said after she'd barked, "Your other right" for what seemed like the hundredth time.

"Nope. It's almost never glamorous. Most of it is knowing your own face and body really well and liking to be the center of attention. If you don't like that, it's a lost cause, believe me."

"You modeled?"

"Yup. Eight years and I hated about seven and a half of them. It paid my bills when I didn't have any other good options, and it paid for me to go to school and buy my first camera. I'm grateful for it. I'm much happier on the other side of the lens, though."

Being the center of attention wasn't something I'd ever sought out, but I wasn't particularly shy either. I was used to paying more attention to other people than they paid to me. But as I looked at Stefan, standing behind Van, watching me, it wasn't a stretch to imagine wanting to be the center of his attention.

His eyes were all over me, roaming my body like he was drinking me in. When he realized I was looking at him he straightened his posture like he was embarrassed at getting caught, and I let a slow grin steal onto my mouth. Might as well make this fun.

I looked at Stefan as if we were in bed and he was naked six inches away from me. His eyes heated in response and I felt a slow tingle of arousal begin deep in my stomach.

"Whatever you're thinking about right now, keep thinking about it," she said, and I heard the shutter click again and again as I changed positions, my eyes never leaving Stefan.

"Stefan, come to my right and keep eye-fucking your boyfriend," Van said a minute later.

"Oh, he's— I— We're—" Stefan spluttered.

"I don't care. Just do it."

Stefan's gaze was hungry, like he could picture everything I wanted to do to him when I got him home. And he'd better believe he was coming home with me after this. I imagined the way his breathing hitched when I sank into his tight ass. The way he keened when I nailed his prostate, as if he was shocked anything could feel so good.

Fuck, I was getting hard picturing him spread out before me, body begging me to take him. But the book in front of my crotch meant that Van couldn't see it, so I let my thoughts run wild.

Stefan on his knees as I fed him my dick. Bending Stefan over in the rooftop garden as I teased his ass, whispering in his ear that anyone could be watching us, then fucking him so hard his come shot all over my vegetable patch. I'd make us dinner with those vegetables after and we'd both taste him in the food. It was filthy and Stefan would hate it. And love it.

I was fully hard now, and my chest felt hot with arousal. I glanced down to see if I was flushed to find my erection poking the pages of the book obscenely.

"I don't care about your dick. Or anyone's dick," Van said. "Almost done."

Relief made me clutch the book a little closer. As it rubbed against the tip of my erection, lust shot through my groin and my eyes fluttered shut. The camera shutter clicked, then the room fell silent.

"Got it," Van said, her voice reverent.

She motioned me over and I froze. It was the oddest version of covering-an-erection-with-a-book-and-getting-called-to-the-front-of-the-class I could imagine. "Um."

Stefan rushed forward with my robe and I locked my eyes on his, then looked down. His quick intake of breath told me he'd seen my hard cock trying to escape from the cock sock.

"That's all for you," I whispered in his ear. He gulped. I tied my robe closed, not that it did much good. Van took one look at me and laughed, shaking her head.

"So epically uninterested," she said. "Don't even worry."

"Thanks."

I turned my attention to the viewfinder and the picture she was showing me. It was in two-thirds profile. My eyes were nearly closed, and my lips were slightly parted. Nipples hard and neck tensed, my hips were flexed toward the book. I looked...obscene. Aroused and private and vulnerable, even though no more skin was showing than I'd bare at the beach.

"Jesus Christ," I muttered, and behind me Stefan's breathing sounded almost choked.

"You look stunning," Van said. "There are other good ones. I'll send you the three I think will work best for the calendar. The final choice is yours, of course, but this one... This is the one, if you ask me."

———

I'D BEEN on the edge of arousal since the photo shoot, and by the time I got my apartment door closed I was desperate. I pressed Stefan against it and kissed him with all the pent-up desire of weeks apart and an hour of edging myself behind a classic of American literature. His arms came around me and his tongue slid against mine, and I was wild with want.

"C'mere," I got out between kisses. "Want you now." I dragged him to the bed while I stripped him and he attempted to fuse us together at the mouth and groin.

My whole body was buzzing and my balls ached with the desire for release, but the second I had Stefan naked on my bed, what I wanted more was to see him come. I wanted him begging and screaming.

With his legs outspread, he gazed up at me, and when he reached a hand out my heart gave a funny little jump. I stripped my own clothes off quickly and lowered myself on top of him.

"Hi," I said, and we both shivered as our erections slid together.

He dragged me down and I slammed my mouth back over

his. We were kissing and grinding against each other and I never wanted to stop.

"Turn over," I told him, slapping his hip lightly. "I want this ass."

Stefan groaned and did as I said. I was pretty sure he had a thing for me talking about his ass, and I was more than happy to oblige.

I squeezed his round cheeks, smooth brown skin irresistible, then dove between them to taste him. His groans as I ate his ass had me all lit up.

"Stop, stop, wait," he moaned, in that voice that meant he was too close to coming. Fuck, it was hot how sensitive he was.

I drew away from him and groaned at what I saw. The globes of his ass gleamed with shimmery green makeup that had rubbed off my face. "Holy shit, your ass looks like pearls." I squeezed the ass in question and Stefan craned around to try and see. The movement must have ground his erection into the bed because he groaned and shivered.

Suddenly I wanted to see his face—*needed* to see his face, so I flipped him over. His gorgeous dick was smeared with precome and when he reached to pull me close, I was on him in a second. I attacked his throat, and kissed up his jaw, and he grabbed my ass, pulling our hips together. By the time my tongue was back in his mouth, we were both so needy we were humping against each other desperately.

"Want to be inside this ass," I growled into his mouth, and he rolled his hips into mine in answer. I made short work of the condom and lube and then I dragged him down the mattress and pushed his knees up, glad he was flexible. He held his legs open for me with a hand under each thigh and I plunged slick fingers inside him. My dick jumped as I watched my fingers open his tight hole.

"Now, now, now," he chanted. On my knees, I touched the

tip of my cock to his hole, teasing the muscle and spreading the lube around.

"You look so damn gorgeous like this," I told Stefan, and his eyes fluttered shut.

He rolled his hips even higher and I couldn't wait one second longer. I lined up and drove myself deep inside him with one thrust.

"Jesus, you feel like fucking heaven," I groaned. Stefan's ass squeezed me so perfectly, and I'd been so on edge, I knew I wasn't going to last long. Fortunately, Stefan seemed to be as desperate as I was.

I started fucking him in long, deep strokes. He had his head thrown back and his fingers were turning white he was gripping his legs so tightly. I slid inside him again, and he clamped around me, crying out.

Pleasure sizzled from my balls to the base of my erection. "Oh, fuck, fuck. Touch yourself, babe, I wanna feel you come on my dick. Wanna watch you blow all over yourself."

Stefan let go with one hand and grabbed his leaking cock, and I started pounding into him. His head snapped back and he screamed, every muscle tightening. Pulse after pulse of come jetted from his dick onto his stomach and chest.

When his ass clamped down on me the thread snapped. The velvet clutch of his body milked my dick until I saw stars. I slammed into him one last time and was gone. My orgasm tore through me and I came so hard my vision went dark.

I let myself collapse onto Stefan, my dick still inside him. His arms came around me and I let out a huge breath of relief, but somehow my hips were still pulsing, tiny shivers of pleasure sizzling up my spine.

I found Stefan's mouth with mine and we kissed lazily, hips moving together. Finally, pleasure turned to overstimulation, and I lowered myself down next to him, exhausted. He was grinning at me.

"You're a total mess right now," I said, nuzzling into his neck. "Covered in come and sparkly makeup." I grinned at the thought.

"You're not exactly shower-fresh yourself," he said, voice hoarse from screaming my name. The satisfaction of it settled over me.

"Well, let's fix that." I rolled upright and held out a hand. "Shower?" He nodded and I pulled him to his feet, holding him close for a moment first.

"That's..." Stefan turned to the beside table where the blue chrysanthemum he'd given me now lived. "You brought it home," he said.

"I, um." I shrugged. "I missed you. I felt terrible that I was such a dick. Guess I wanted something of you here in case I never saw you again."

He ran a gentle fingertip over the chrysanthemum's petals, as if saying hello, then he slid his hand into mine.

We kissed under the hot water, and I took advantage of the opportunity to touch every inch of him. He returned the favor and it resulted in a lazy jerk-off session, both of us finally wrung dry.

Happy and satisfied, we trooped back into my bedroom hand in hand, and I offered him some sweats. He took them from me slowly like they were a curiosity. To him, they probably were. He probably had matching pajama sets or fancy boxers engineered for sleep.

I tugged on my sweats and an old T-shirt from a BBG fundraising night years before. Stefan followed my lead, but he was still shivering so I grabbed him my hoodie. When his head popped through the neck hole, he looked like a different person. He looked...adorable.

"I like you in my clothes," I said. It was a drastic under-statement.

STEFAN

"I FEEL RIDICULOUS," I told Milo, looking down at the baggy gray sweatpants and bleach-stained navy blue hooded sweatshirt. But when I took a deep breath, I could smell Milo all around me, so maybe these clothes weren't the worst thing.

"You look gorgeous," he said. And for once, it wasn't flirtatious or sexual. It was just appreciative.

"Thank you." I cleared my throat and tried to figure out where to begin, because now that we weren't having sex, the awkwardness crept in.

"Wanna go to the roof?" He was already looking out the window.

"You must go absolutely stir-crazy in the winter. What do you do when it's too cold to be outside all the time?"

"I just go outside anyway," Milo said, and shrugged, like it was the most obvious thing in the world.

And maybe it was. If you liked something—loved something; needed it—you found a way to have it. Heavy coat, hat and gloves, you found a way. Wasn't it a lot like what I did in my lab? Finding a way for things that didn't naturally go together to thrive anyway.

The lemony sun of early evening made the greenery glow

and cast deep shadows, like a garden in negative. Milo slid two beers from the pockets of his sweatpants and winked at me.

"Listen," he said, squaring his shoulders. "I said it before, but I need to say it again. I'm sorry about how I handled it when you told me about your promotion opportunity." He glanced up at me and grimaced. "I *did* mean what I said, but I said it in a dick way."

He ran a hand through his damp curls, and his expression turned uncertain.

"I think partly I heard you say that you would be busier and I had this reaction like, you'd never have time to hang out with me again." He rolled his eyes. "I'm pathetic, huh?"

The same heat I'd felt each time I got one of Milo's texts suffused me. "No. The idea that you'd want to spend your time with me is not pathetic. It's...amazing."

Milo tangled our fingers together, his grin bright and unworried. "Okay, cool," he said, and I shook my head at him, but I couldn't help but smile back.

"I really do love my job. I know you think it's soulless or boring, but...I don't know how to explain it exactly. The biology of plants—it's like a puzzle. How they've adapted to certain environments, in certain places. And taking that apart, reducing them down to their component elements, and seeing how I can put them back together...it's like learning how the world works all over again, every time."

Milo's fingers tightened around mine.

"And I like working in the lab, usually. I like the quiet, the solitude. I find it meditative. But...I think I might like it even better if I knew I would have some...not quiet, non-solitude later."

"'Not quiet, non-solitude,' right here," Milo said, pointing at himself and grinning. "Seriously, though, I don't think your job's soulless, and I do want to know more about it."

I thought of all the resources I had at my disposal in the lab, of all the knowledge contained there, and of how comparatively little we shared it.

"I was thinking, actually. That maybe there's a way we could...collaborate. If you wanted. I thought I could write a proposal to offer an internship at the lab. Open it up to students like the ones from Erasmus, who have an interest in botany. The ones who are interested in the lab side of things, that is."

Milo's eyes widened. "That would be amazing. Because the thing is that some of the kids are more like you, you know? They'd love the chance to do more of the bio side of things, but there's no funding for that kind of lab resources in the public school system, and—"

"I know," I said.

"But it would have to be a paid internship, you know, otherwise kids who need to get a job to help out their families wouldn't be able to apply, which just totally echoes the—"

"I know," I said, and I kissed him. "I thought maybe you could help me with the proposal."

Milo opened his mouth, then snapped it shut and nodded happily.

He leaned in and kissed me again, and I twined my fingers into his hair, enjoying the heat of his mouth and the cool weight of his damp curls.

Milo broke the kiss to point, and I saw the first cat of the night—a small calico this time—creeping toward the catnip.

"That's Tiny Shells," Milo said. "She's grouchy and awesome. She sleeps standing up but the second you get near her, she wakes up and glares at you."

"Tiny Shells?"

"Yeah, cuz calico looks like tortoiseshell, and the mac-and-cheese shape is tiny shells, and she's little, you know?"

I cupped his face. "You're very strange."

He winked at me and leered. We watched Tiny Shells in

silence for a while, holding hands. It was the most at peace I'd ever felt.

"So, you and me," Milo said. "We're gonna...try? Being together? Or, ooh, taking over the world together, one botany lab and community garden at a time?"

I knew he was kidding—probably. But hearing him talk about us being a team, working on something we both cared about together? It was everything I'd always wanted and never thought I'd have.

"I want that," I said, my voice soft and a little shaky. "I really want that." I cleared my throat. "You know, we're probably going to keep disagreeing about the value of certain botanical approaches over others."

"I hope so," Milo said. "I hope we keep fighting about it for a long, long time." And he shot me the filthiest grin I'd ever seen, but his hands on my face were sweet. "That way we can keep making up."

EPILOGUE

STEFAN

TWO MONTHS later

I WAS EARLY AS USUAL, so I got to watch Milo arrive, unseen. Leaning against a thornless honey maple, I saw him the second he turned the corner and loped toward me. With his rolling gait and wild dark curls, he was the picture of easy confidence. His brown skin gleamed against the white of his T-shirt and his sinewy arms were on display, hands shoved in the pockets of the worn jeans that made his ass look amazing.

I still couldn't believe that he was mine. That I could reach out and wind one of his curls around my finger, or kiss his smirking mouth. That I got to argue with him about going to the store or letting the roof cats inside or eating pizza for breakfast. That I fell asleep with him and woke up with him. And that sometimes when I woke in the middle of the night and worried that he would become bored with me, he kissed me until I couldn't think, and then fell asleep on top of me, tangled up so tight all my fears were assuaged.

Most of all, I still couldn't believe the way his face lit up when he noticed me—as if just by being there, I made everything better. Like now. When he caught sight of me, he grinned hugely and jerked his chin at me.

"Hey, you're Stef-on-time," he said, which meant "early."

"Yeah, it was so nice I walked from—"

He pressed me against the honey maple and kissed me before I could finish my sentence. I'd long ago decided that Milo's mouth felt better than just about everything. Now he tasted of coffee and the spearmint he plucked off a plant in the BBG and chewed.

"Rude," I murmured against his soft lips. He nodded his agreement, gave me one last kiss, and straightened my shirt where he'd mussed me.

"Okay, let's do this." He slid his hand into mine and pulled me after him.

It was basically what he'd been doing since we met. But I'd learned to pull him along, too, the last two months.

It hadn't always been easy. When I was offered the promotion at Scion, we fought bitterly, at first about the work itself, but it soon became clear that it was a fight about what kind of future we might have.

Milo had showed up at my apartment early the next morning, looking like he hadn't slept. He'd flopped down on my couch and glared, and finally said that he worried if I took the promotion I wouldn't have time to see him anymore, or free time to come work with the kids at the BBG.

He'd said because he'd always just casually hooked up with friends he'd never worried that he wouldn't have enough time with someone before. He'd never wished they could be together all the time.

He'd glared through the whole monologue like he resented

every word, but in the end, he'd told me that he loved me, so *duh*, he didn't want me wasting away in some laboratory tower where he'd never see me. He'd glared through every word of that too, and for the first time, I'd seen how scared he was. Scared to depend on anyone other than himself. Scared to think that another person's opinion or schedule or desires could control him. Scared that someone might care less than he did.

We'd talked all day, until Milo fell asleep with his head in my lap and a pizza crust on his chest, and we'd worked out where we stood.

I set up a meeting with Dr. Sorenson the next day, and offered a way to restructure the time I'd spend at Scion if I took on the added responsibilities I'd applied for, and explained that I had developed a newfound interest in combining my scientific research with more local applications. In the end, Dr. Sorenson decided to give the promotion to one of my colleagues, but approved the plan I proposed to use some of Scion's research monies to establish a paid summer internship for a high school student interested in using botanical research to benefit their community. Milo worked with me the whole way, to get it up and running.

———

WE CUT through the alleyway and walked through a small back gate, and the smells of the city gave way to freshly turned earth and sun-warmed plants. In the end, the Erasmus students had flipped the script on Milo just like I had on Dr. Sorenson, deciding that rather than just taking their plants back to their own neighborhoods, they would collaborate on a community garden that could house vegetables, flowers, herbs, and everything in between.

We wended our way through the raised beds and found the Erasmus students with their friends and families near the newly erected fence at the entrance to the garden. Deon was wrapping a thick red ribbon across the entrance and Sonja was laughing at him.

The sign on the fence above the ribbon read *Moss Smoothie Community Garden*.

Abraham waved as we approached, and Troy nodded at us before standing quietly near the fence. I still hadn't heard Troy say more than a few words, but Milo had convinced him to stay on at the BBG after the Erasmus program ended and learn more about horticulture. He said Troy had smiled bigger than he'd ever seen when he told him.

Everyone else turned to greet us. Milo shook hands with a lot of parents who thanked him for working with their kids and a few more who seemed not to know why they were there and hoped whatever it was would end quickly. Rooney had wrestled a few two-liters of soda from the nearby bodega, so we drank a toast to Moss Smoothie Community Garden, and cheered as Sonja held up the scissors she'd use to cut the ribbon.

"I want to thank Milo for getting those stupid people to let us use this lot." She raised her cup of soda to him. "I just think it's cool we did this together," she said to her friends. "I think probably I'll walk by here a lot and look in and just know that we made this, and that we can do that. Make things. Change shit. Stuff, I mean," she amended at a glare from a woman who looked like she might be her mother. "Makes it seem like we could do it again and again. Then do it somewhere else until a lot of shi—*stuff*'s different. Anyway."

She rolled her eyes and threw back the rest of her soda.

"Should I do this?" She held up the scissors.

"Wait one sec," Milo said. He pushed me forward.

I was nervous, suddenly, though I'd known these kids for months now. Last night, I'd agonized over what to say and Milo had elbowed me in the ribs and told me to keep it short and sweet because it wasn't about me and no one liked speeches.

"I'm happy to be able to announce the recipient of the first ever Scion Laboratory summer internship today. We had twenty-eight impressive applications, but the committee has chosen Deon White!"

I lifted my plastic cup to Deon whose eyes got huge and mouth fell open.

"Seriously?" he said.

"Come on, bro, you know Stefan doesn't make jokes," Abraham said, and everyone nodded like this was obvious. Milo grinned and winked at me.

"Seriously," I confirmed, ignoring them.

"Wow," was all Deon said. I shook his hand and he squeezed mine, and didn't have to say anything.

Milo slid his arm around my waist and kissed my ear. "You're fucking awesome," he said, and I could feel his smile.

Sonja dragged Deon up to cut the ribbon with her, making fun of how old school it was the whole time.

The scissors sliced through the ribbon and the sun shone down on the kids' happy faces and I pulled Milo close to me, breathing in the scents of dirt and plants and the man I loved.

THE END

———

BINGE A NEW SERIES NOW!

A RELUCTANT ROCK STAR, a musician struggling with demons, a couple battling the ghosts of the past, a couple trying to make a future. They're all in the **RIVEN** series!

EXCERPT FROM RIVEN

"Theo Decker: Reluctant Rock Star."

That was the headline that accompanied the cover of *Groove* magazine that came out today, and it was the reason I was hiding in my dressing room from the rest of the band. I could already imagine Ven, nostrils flaring, voice tight with anger: *Lead singer standing in for the whole band again, awesome!*

And that was before you even got to the photo, which was about fifty percent me.

I pulled the magazine out of my bag to glare at it and my stomach dropped again. Ven, Coco, and Ethan hovered in the background, eclipsed by me. My arms were wrapped around myself like a straitjacket or a hug and I was gazing up at the camera in what had been an awkward plea for the shoot to be over, but looked coy. I cursed myself for the hundredth time for believing the smarmy editor who'd assured me that of course all the band members would be featured equally.

Reluctant rock star wasn't precisely accurate. More like, Rock Star Who Loves Performing with a Fiery Passion but Hates Being Famous More than He Ever Expected. Only that didn't make for a very snappy headline.

I cast one last look in the dressing room mirror. Staring back at me wasn't a rock star of any description. It was a scared kid who'd gone from no one caring about him to everyone caring about him in the time it would take most people to clean out a garage. My black hair was wild around my face, just like it always was, gray eyes ringed in days of overlaid black eyeliner, just like they always were, lips bitten raw, as had become common lately. My black jeans were tight, permanently sweat-creased behind the knees, and hanging a little low on my hips, since I hadn't been able to stomach much lately. The white T-shirt hung on me, making my arms look skinnier than they were, and my shoulders sharper.

It wasn't even a costume. These were my own clothes, my own aesthetic, just as I used my real name. Which made it feel even weirder to see it all turned into a persona. Theo Decker: Reluctant Rock Star.

I smeared on some lip balm so my mouth wouldn't crack and bleed onstage, hitched my jeans up, and patted the lucky pick I wore on a string around my neck, hidden under my T-shirt. The one I'd been using the night Ethan had heard me at Sushi Bar's open mic night and changed my life forever. I hummed a few lines of our opening song. My voice was on its last legs, but this was the end of the tour, thank God, and I'd have time to rest it.

I swallowed hard, pushing the sick feeling of alienation from the rest of Riven down into the pit of my stomach.

"Okay, *go*," I ordered Theo Decker in the mirror, and pushed through the door to join my band.

Blinded by floodlights, shaky with exertion, and high on adrenaline, I closed my eyes as the lights changed for our final song. It had been a great set, the rest of the band coming through despite their anger at the cover, just like I knew they would. They always did. We were magical together. That's what everybody said. Synergistic. Nearly psychic.

Coco plucked the first, haunting notes of "No More Time," our newest single, as the stage washed in eerie blue light. They reverberated, striking like a gong in my chest. Ven came in with the bass line, then Ethan counted in, and the rhythm went to double time. I pounded the drumbeats with my foot, needing to wring every last bit of energy out onto the stage.

There was this moment, before the first note left my mouth, when everything changed. There was the before and the after; the quiet and the noise; the off and the on. It was the moment when I felt like I appeared, pushing everything that I was out of myself like the notes I sang were a strong-currented river, able to disgorge me.

I'd written this song in about twenty minutes. It had fallen into my head fully formed, like something in a dream. It swooped and soared from the bottom of my register to the top, and there was a moment after the second bridge when the instruments cut out and I hit a note that blasted through the sudden silence like a wrecking ball.

Tonight, since I knew it was the last show of the tour, I sang it with everything I had left, let it pull me to my tiptoes and to the edge of the stage, sweat flicking off my hair as I threw myself open before the screaming crowd.

The crowd. They thundered around me, their stomps and screams like my own heartbeat, their energy coursing through me like blood. These were the moments I lived for. These were the moments that made every other miserable bit of fame worth it.

I opened my arms, threw my head back, and shattered myself to pieces for them, until there was nothing left.

"It's a phenomenal opportunity—a real honor," Dougal, our manager, was saying as we sat in Coco's dressing room after the show. I was so exhausted I was hardly listening to him. Still floaty from performing, I was already gone, back to New York and my apartment, blissfully alone.

"It would just mean extending by three more weeks. Easy-peasy."

My blitzed brain caught on the absurdity of "easy-peasy," before it got around to processing the rest of his sentence.

"Extending?" I croaked around my cherry menthol cough drop.

"Just for three weeks or so," Dougal confirmed. "The Scandinavian leg of the tour would end the first day of the DeadBeat Festival. Done."

I looked around at the rest of the band, expecting to see that they were equally horrified at the idea of extending the tour. But Coco looked excited, her foot tapping like it always did when she was plotting; Ethan was nodding, and Ven had leaned forward, elbows on knees.

My heart began to triphammer and suddenly the taste of the cherry threatened to make me sick. I shook my head.

"You guys, no way. I can't." My throat felt raw, a metallic taste lurking beneath the cherry and menthol.

"But, the DeadBeat Festival!" Coco crowed, at the same time Ven said, "It's a major ask, and major sales after the festival."

Coco shot him a look, as if they'd already discussed the tack they were going to take and that wasn't it. *Had* they discussed it? Had Dougal told them but not me? She went on, "Cavalcade and The Runny Whites are playing. DJ Romulus is gonna be there. If it'd make people think of us as being in the same league as artists like them, how can we turn it down? Besides, it's only three more weeks. What's three weeks after four months?"

Ven, Ethan, and Dougal nodded their agreement and my heart sank.

This date marked in my calendar had been the only thing getting me through the last month. The Boston show meant the end of the tour. The promise of home, of the familiar streets of my neighborhood, the warmth and solitude of my own bed, and the chance to just . . . *be,* without being under constant scrutiny. I longed for it.

But I couldn't say any of that to the band. They had been living for this tour. After all, it was what they'd always been working toward—long before they'd met me.

I was opening my mouth to say that I just didn't have another three weeks left in me, when Ven fixed me with a cool stare.

"Come on, bro. Everyone says you're the star. Well, stars have to pay their dues."

And there it was. They were all looking at me. Coco's expression was pleading, Ethan's hopeful, Ven's a challenge, and Dougal's the studied neutrality of calculation.

"You all want to?" I asked them, and was immediately met with a chorus of yeses.

"I—"

How could I let them down? We were a team; we were supposed to look out for each other. Usually, we were friends, too. I needed to be on the same side as them or being in Riven was beyond lonely. If I said no, I ruined it for all of them. Besides, Coco was right about what it meant for us to be asked to play the festival, to be asked to add dates to our tour. It meant we'd arrived.

If only I wanted to be at the place where we'd arrived.

"Okay," I said, my voice a whisper. "Sure. It's only three weeks."

We had a day and a half back in New York to gather our stuff before flying to Europe. It was just enough time to be reminded of all the ways that tour wasn't real life, but not enough to actually feel rested before leaving again. The second the car dropped me at my apartment I fell into bed, so relieved to know that no one would knock on my door or try to interrupt me that I slept for hours before waking, ravenous, around 10 p.m.

119

I felt almost human again after a quick shower and a quick bowl of pho at the Vietnamese restaurant around the corner from my apartment, the one where I could sit at the counter with my back to the other diners and my hat pulled low, so no one could recognize me. Since it was late, I decided it was safe to brave a walk after I ate.

One of the worst things about being recognizable was that I practically had to run a recon mission just to know if it was safe to grab a damn slice of pizza. I couldn't pop out for a bite or go to a movie without risking being set upon by people snapping pictures or grabbing at me. I had to know the places where I could hide in plain sight, like the Vietnamese restaurant, or enter through an alleyway to avoid a crowd. More often than not, I didn't even bother, because getting caught in a flurry of photos and whispers left me frazzled, drained, and too anxious to want the pizza or the movie by the time the crowd had passed.

But tonight there was a gorgeous bloom of fresh spring air, and by the time I got back from the new leg of this tour, it would be summer, that edge of cool breeze rustling the leaves gone, replaced by the smell of garbage and too many bodies. So I walked. In the dark, with my hat shading my eyes, in my jeans, Chucks, and T-shirt, I looked like a hundred other dudes.

I walked aimlessly at first, relishing the simple pleasure of letting my mind wander after months of fretting over details, always with somewhere to be. But as anxious thoughts about the next few weeks intruded, I turned east and headed over the Brooklyn Bridge. I'd done it a hundred times, but pausing in the middle of the bridge, looking back toward Manhattan and out toward the Statue of Liberty, always felt special. The wind from the water whipped my hair and I stuffed my hat in my back pocket so it wouldn't get blown off, and pulled my jean jacket on. I was always cold these days, except when I was onstage.

I'd had no idea what it would feel like to perform—really

perform, the crowd so loud and the stage so large that every step, every note, every gesture, was a show.

The first time I'd realized it, we were opening for Oops Icarus. It was our first tour, our first show. The rest of the band was nervous that people wouldn't know who we were, but I felt liberated by the relative anonymity. It was easier to believe this was just an experiment, and that if it failed, I wouldn't be that loser, Theo, who dropped out of college for a pipe dream, like my parents said. When we ripped into our first song, I felt the prickle of all my senses coming alive. For once, I didn't feel like gawky Theo who cared too much about the music.

I sang with everything I had, hair lashing my face, sweat gathering at the backs of my knees and trickling down my spine. When we ran offstage at the end of our set, Coco's eyes were wide and Ven was looking at me with a grudging respect I'd never seen from him. Ethan clapped me on the back. That was when I knew they hadn't expected me to be that good, that they'd needed me for the songs I could provide, without thinking about what it would be like to have me around. It took the wind out of me, since they'd pursued me for the band single-mindedly.

When I first met them, it felt like I finally belonged some-where—was *wanted* somewhere—for the first fucking time in my life. Onstage that first time, under the hot lights and the ringing in my ears, with dust motes forming a constellation that connected me with the audience as if we could stay suspended in it forever, I felt it for the second time.

I belonged onstage. I *was* wanted, there. By the band, by the audience. And, most surprisingly, by myself. I could lose myself in a way I'd never known, and by losing myself I found pieces I could live with.

And it's what I came back to every time I thought all the rest of it wasn't worth it. Onstage, I felt invincible, but also so, so open. It was the impossibility of the combination that made it so potent. Onstage, I was blown open, but held.

Prospect Heights was turning into Crown Heights, and I was thinking of heading home, back to bed, when I heard something that stopped me dead on the sidewalk.

The back door of a bar was flung open to the spring night, and inside, someone was playing a song that sent shivers all through me. It was mournful and angry and beautiful and raw, and the feelings of it roiled around in my chest until I was craning to hear more. I couldn't see who was playing, so I walked around to the front door, expecting a crowd, but the place was nearly empty, just a couple of randoms scattered around the bar.

And there he was. Back turned to the room, a man played guitar and sang under his breath, voice whiskey low and honey sweet. No crowd, no audience, he was playing for himself, one foot resting on the rung of a beat-up chair, tattooed fingers cradling his guitar like a precious thing. The notes he tore from that guitar twisted me up and set me buzzing with energy, like they were seeping into my skin.

Before I was even aware I'd moved, I found myself beside him.

"Sorry," I said when he stiffened and turned, sensing he was no longer alone.

When he faced me, I swallowed hard. He looked like I'd pulled him back from someplace far away. But goddamn, was he gorgeous.

He was taller than me, broad and thick with muscle, but his fingers on the guitar were poetry. Intense dark eyes—brown or maybe a dark green—beneath expressive eyebrows, brown hair combed back, full mouth surrounded by a groomed beard. He looked like some half-mad sea captain who'd wandered ashore.

"Help you, bro?" he drawled.

I couldn't remember the last time I'd approached a stranger.

Nowadays, people usually approached me and I tried to avoid them, and before . . . it wasn't that I was shy, exactly, I just never assumed people would welcome my approach.

"Is that yours? The song."

He nodded.

I'm obsessed with it. The expression dropped into my head, what I used to say about songs, books, movies I felt a kind of connection with that I couldn't quite explain because it seemed in excess of the thing itself.

"I love it," I said. It sounded trite and generic but I couldn't have meant it more. The guy raised an eyebrow. Not unkind, just not very enthusiastic.

"Thanks, man."

Then he started to turn away and I felt a dire need to prevent it. Because, after months on tour, with music feeling oppressive, the joy that song called forth in me was such a welcome relief—such a gift—I couldn't let it go. And if he turned away, the tendril connecting me to this moment would snap, and I'd careen off into space. Back out into the dark night; back to my empty apartment; back on tour to day after day of nameless, interchangeable cities and night after night of nameless, interchangeable men.

I put a hand out, plucked at his sleeve. It was a red, waffle-knit Henley that fit him close to the skin, so what I'd intended as an impersonal touch instead let me feel the warmth of his body, the strength of his muscles, sinewy beneath the worn fabric. His nostrils flared and his eyes narrowed slightly.

"That part after the bridge, where it seemed like you were gonna go up but then you dropped into minor. How'd you choose that?"

After a pause that stretched long enough I thought he wasn't going to answer, he shrugged and said, "Just tried it a couple different ways. Liked that one best."

But I didn't believe him. That unexpected key change—

going down instead of up—it was masterful. Unique and haunting and . . . accomplished. No way was this guy just playing around for fun.

"It changed the whole mood of the song," I ventured. "It was sad, longing. But then that one moment made the whole thing feel, like, eerie. Haunted and . . ."

I shrugged, irritated by how uncertain I sounded. I *knew* music. Music was the one thing I could talk about with anyone. So why did I feel like every sentence carried an incredible weight?

"Yeah, that's right," the guy said, voice warming slightly. "I didn't want to let the listener just be sad. Too easy. Too comfortable. It had to spin them around a little. Make them question what they'd felt so far."

His eyes burned into me as he talked, voice low and rumbling as thunder, catching at the lowest notes. I tried to think of something to say, but my brain and my voice were gone, lost somewhere in his eyes and his words, and I just looked at him. Finally, I forced myself to look down because I was probably creeping the guy out.

"I'm Theo."

"Hey, Theo. Caleb."

He reached for my hand as if the idea of an introduction without a handshake was unthinkable, even in a dirty bar. I could feel the calluses on the tips of his fingers, and his hand was rough and dry. He wore a ring on the middle finger, a thick, smooth band of metal that looked like the kind of thing you never take off.

The hand I was holding had strummed that beautiful song out of his guitar, and I wanted to squeeze it so tight that some of that magic leached into me. I wanted to pull its beauty inside me.

READ RIVEN NOW!

DEAR READER,

Thank you so much for reading ***Natural Enemies***! I hope you enjoyed Stefan and Milo's story.

If you did, consider spreading the word! You can help others find this book by writing reviews, blogging about it, and talking about it on social media. Reviews and shares really help authors keep writing, and we appreciate them so much! The power is in your hands.

Thank you!

xo, Roan Parrish

Want to get exclusive content and news of future book releases? Sign up for my **newsletter** on my website, **roanparrish.com**!

ABOUT THE AUTHOR

Roan Parrish lives in Philadelphia where she is gradually attempting to write love stories in every genre.

When not writing, she can usually be found cutting her friends' hair, meandering through whatever city she's in while listening to torch songs and melodic death metal, or cooking overly elaborate meals. She loves bonfires, winter beaches, minor chord harmonies, and self-tattooing. One time she may or may not have baked a six-layer chocolate cake and then thrown it out the window in a fit of pique.

MORE INFORMATION

Keep up with all my new releases and get exclusive free content by signing up for my **NEWSLETTER** at **roanparrish.com**.

Come join **PARRISH OR PERISH**, my Facebook group, to hang out, chat about books, and get exclusive news, updates, excerpts of works in progress, freebies, and pictures of my cat!

You can follow me on **BOOKBUB** and **AMAZON** to find out when my books are on sale.

You can follow me on **PINTEREST** at ARoanParrish, to see visuals of all my characters, books, and settings. And you can follow me on **TWITTER**, **FACEBOOK**, and **INSTAGRAM** at RoanParrish.

IN THE MIDDLE OF
SOMEWHERE
Roan Parrish

OUT OF
NOWHERE
Roan Parrish

MIDDLE of
SOMEWHERE
BOOK 2

WHERE WE
LEFT OFF
Roan Parrish

MIDDLE of
SOMEWHERE
BOOK 3

SMALL
CHANGE
ROAN PARRISH

INVITATION
TO THE
BLUES
ROAN PARRISH

HEART of the STEAL

AVON GALE
ROAN PARRISH

The
Remaking
of
Corbin
Wale

ROAN PARRISH

NATURAL
ENEMIES

ROAN PARRISH

THRALL

AVON GALE &
ROAN PARRISH

RIVEN
ROAN PARRISH

REND
ROAN PARRISH

RAVE
ROAN PARRISH

ALSO BY ROAN PARRISH

The Middle of Somewhere Series:

In the Middle of Somewhere

Out of Nowhere

Where We Left Off

The Small Change Series:

Small Change

Invitation to the Blues

The Riven Series:

Riven

Rend

Raze

The Remaking of Corbin Wale

Natural Enemies

Heart of the Steal (with Avon Gale)

Thrall (with Avon Gale

MORE INFORMATION ABOUT PLANT-BASED SOCIAL JUSTICE

Are you interested in learning more about the ways that growing can have positive impacts in our communities? Below are links to a number of farms, seed-saving projects, markets, and food justice programs. Check out all the amazing work that people like Milo are doing!

Black Urban Growers: Black Urban Growers (BUGS) is an organization committed to building networks and community support for growers in both urban and rural settings.

Detroit Black Food Sovereignty Network: The Detroit Black Community Food Security Network (DBCFSN) was formed in February 2006 to address food insecurity in Detroit's Black community, and to organize members of that community to play a more active leadership role in the local food security movement.

Earth's Keepers: Earth's Keepers is an urban farm dedicated to bringing healthy, organic, affordable produce to the West Philadelphia community.

East New York Farms!: The mission of the East New York Farms Project is to organize youth and adults to address food justice in our community by promoting local sustainable agriculture and community-led economic development.

Farm School NYC: Farm School NYC trains local residents in urban agriculture in order to build self-reliant communities and inspire positive local action around food access and social, economic, and racial justice issues.

Food First: The Institute for Food and Development Policy, better known as Food First, works to end the injustices that cause hunger through research, education and action.

Just Food: Just Food galvanizes engaged individuals to develop thriving communities that have the power to feed, educate, and advocate for each other. They envision a sovereign and healthy food system rooted in racial, social, economic, and environmental justice.

Native American Food Sovereignty Alliance: NAFSA is dedicated to restoring, supporting and developing Indigenous food systems through best practices and advocacy that place Indigenous peoples at the center of national, Tribal and local policies and natural resources management to ensure food security and health of all future generations.

Philly Urban Creators: The Urban Creators is a grassroots organization rooted in North Philadelphia, transforming neglected landscapes into dynamic safe-spaces that foster connectivity, self-sufficiency, and innovation. They are community organizers who utilize urban agriculture, interest-based learning, artistic expression, restorative justice, and celebration as tools for neighborhood stabilization and youth development.

Resilient Roots Farm: Resilient Roots Garden (a project of Vietlead) is an intergenerational community garden that provides high school internships.

Rise & Root Farm: Rise & Root is a cooperatively run farm in the black dirt region of Orange County, New York. Their farm team is made of strong women, teachers, leaders, students, and growers. They grow vegetables, flowers, and herbs using sustainable growing techniques—they never use chemical pesticides or herbicides on their farm. Instead, they focus on building up a healthy ecosystem and restoring balance to the land.

Soil Generation: Soil Generation is a Black & Brown-led coalition of gardeners, farmers, individuals, and community-based organizations working to ensure people of color regain community control of land and food, to secure access to the resources necessary to determine how the land is used, address community health concerns, grow food and improve the environment.

Soul Fire Farm: Soul Fire Farm is committed to ending racism and injustice in the food system. We raise life-giving food and act in solidarity with people marginalized by food apartheid.

The Southern Sustainable Agriculture Working Group: Southern SAWG was founded in 1991 to foster a movement towards a more sustainable farming and food system—one that is ecologically sound, economically viable, socially just and humane. They function as a regional entity, working with and through hundreds of associated organizations across 13 southern states. By building partnerships, sharing information and conducting analysis, they transform isolated ideas and innovations into practical tools and approaches for widespread use.

Truelove Seeds: Truelove Seeds offers rare, open pollinated, and culturally important vegetable, herb, and flower seeds grown by urban and rural farmers committed to community food sovereignty and sustainable agriculture.

Wildseed: Wildseed is an emerging Black and Brown-led, feminine-centered, queer-loving, earth-based intentional community, organic farm, healing sanctuary, and political and creative home forming on 181 acres in Millerton, NY, two hours north of NYC.

Made in the USA
Las Vegas, NV
01 March 2021

18864592R00083